SHARED FOR THE SHEIKH

A NOVEL BY

ANNABELLE WINTERS

Books by Annabelle Winters

The CURVES FOR SHEIKHS Series

Curves for the Sheikh
Flames for the Sheikh
Hostage for the Sheikh
Single for the Sheikh
Stockings for the Sheikh
Untouched for the Sheikh
Surrogate for the Sheikh
Stars for the Sheikh
Shelter for the Sheikh
Shared for the Sheikh

Shared for the Sheikh

A NOVEL BY

Annabelle Winters

2018
Rainshine Books
USA

Copyright Notice

SHARED FOR THE SHEIKH

1

Professor Janice Johansen. It sounded nice, didn't it? Much better than the cumbersome Associate Professor or the lame-ass Assistant Professor or the mortifying title of Lecturer, which pretty much meant you were never going to get tenure.

Not that Jan had gotten that coveted tenured title yet. Yes, all indications were that the board would vote to grant her tenure at the end of the year, but it was never a sure thing. After all American universities waived the retirement age, tenured positions were hard to come by. You pretty much had to wait for one of the old guard to actually die at his desk for a spot to open up!

"This is your year, Jan," she said to herself as she checked her look in her iPhone camera. "This research you're doing will be the jewel in your crown, and when it's published, they'll be begging you to accept tenure out of fear of losing you to one of those fancy Ivy League schools."

Not that she wanted to leave the University of Pittsburgh. Jan was a Pennsylvania girl: Dutch, German, and maybe some Cherokee mixed in. Who knew. Who cared. She'd never been particularly curious about her ethnicity, never wanted to do those in-vogue ancestry tests. Genetics wasn't her thing, even though her PhD was in Biology and she'd been hired into the Biology Department. Her research interests had trended more towards sociology—how people lived together in societies large and small, ancient and modern, past and present. How they lived to-gether, and how they . . . well, how they . . .

"Good morning, I'm Dr. Janice Johansen from the University of Pittsburgh," she said in the privacy of the single-person restroom she'd found somewhere in the maze of hallways that crisscrossed the conference wing of the Dubai Metropolitan Palace Hotel in the heart of the United Arab Emirates. "And I'm study-ing alternative marital structures and socio-sexual arrangements in modern societies, contrasting and comparing them with our primitive ancestors, who lived in small hunter-gatherer tribes in which most adults practiced shared sexual relationships as a way to strengthen the bonds between . . ." She trailed off and shook her head when she considered that the men and women at the conference—assuming there would even be any women in the room—were mostly wealthy Arabs, all of them millionaires, sev-eral of them billionaires, and some of them straight-up, honest-to-goodness royalty. Most of them would be followers of conservative Islam, but they weren't uneducated fools. Many of the younger Arabs had spent time in the West, studying or partying or doing multi-million-dollar business deals. They were used to Americans trying to make things sound more important and serious than they were, and they'd immediately see through her well-rehearsed academic nonsense.

"Maybe it's better to just say it in plain English," she muttered as she dabbed at a smudge on her lipstick, wondering why she was doing her face on her iPhone camera when there was a mirror in front of her. Perhaps it was because she had the camera permanently switched to the soft light effect, which smoothed out her skin and made her look younger. All those late nights studying in college, six years in grad school, and then another God-knows-how-many years at Pitt teaching and doing research had taken a toll on Jan, as her mother always pointed out.

"You should have started with the deep-wrinkle treatment in your twenties," Mother Johansen had said the previous Christmas when she'd inspected Jan's face with a frown, running her bony finger along Jan's forehead and then tapping her twice between the eyes like she was trying to release an evil spirit who was causing wrinkles to appear. "You can't suddenly decide to start taking care of your skin when you're in your thirties and expect to look presentable."

"Wait, are you saying I'm so wrinkled that I'm not presentable?" Jan had snapped, every tiny muscle in her face tensing up as it occurred to her that ninety-percent of the few wrinkles she had were the result of the two weeks a year she spent with Mom. "Should I sit at the table with a bag over my head? Or maybe I just stay in the kitchen while your presentable friends gather around the tree and Botox each other into oblivion."

Mom's expression would have changed if not for the recent Botox session, and Jan had smirked and shaken her head and pushed her glasses firmly up against her nose. Jan knew Mom hated the fact that she wore glasses. Maybe that's why she'd never switched to contacts. Who knew.

"Firstly," Mom had said curtly. "They're not friends, they're family. My family and your family."

Jan had taken a breath and turned away. The "family" Mom was talking about were the step-kids of her third husband, with whom she'd eloped, which meant Jan hadn't been invited to the wedding, which meant there wasn't really a wedding, as far as Jan was concerned. And the step-kids? Well, they weren't "kids." They were all in their thirties and some had step-kids of their own. So with all of that, Jan couldn't keep it straight and didn't really want to. And no, the irony didn't escape her that now she was somehow fascinated with studying "alternative" family and marital structures across the world when she could write a goddamn book about the nonsense going on in her own mother's kitchen.

"Breathe," she told herself, finally turning to the mirror. She shifted uncomfortably in her skirt-suit, which had become alarmingly tight since she'd last worn it a year earlier. Perhaps it was all that sugary tea and sweet dates she'd been eating while in the Middle East. Or perhaps she was just destined to be fat, she told herself, trying to feel sorry for herself in that perverse way she did sometimes. It didn't work. Jan had too much of a sense of self-worth to feel down about having a big butt.

Back in those primitive societies a large woman was a coveted prize, she reminded herself. Girth and heft was a signal of health and fertility, not to mention wealth and status. Yes. Tell yourself that, hold your boobs up right, stick your fat ass out like you're proud, and walk out there with your glasses and your theories. Shake hands with these Sheikhs, and get them to talk about what you're here to learn about: Polygamy.

Polygamy. The disgusting, misogynistic, oppressive practice of a man taking multiple wives. Sure, a self-proclaimed prophet in Utah could take a hundred wives while these Sheikhs were only allowed four by Islamic law, but these weren't madmen living on rural farms in the middle of nowhere. And the wom-

en weren't sheltered know-nothings either: Indeed,
Jan knew that many western-educated Arab wom-
en of royal blood willingly entered into such appall-
ing arrangements even when they had the choice of
stepping away from tradition. Was it brainwashing?
Abuse? Or was there something deep in human nature that said sharing a spouse is perhaps not as evil
as we'd like to think, was perhaps more common in
our past than we'd like to admit? That's what Jan
was here to find out. Real interviews. Real data. The
old ways were slowly dying out even in the conservative Middle East, she knew, and within a couple of
generations the practice of polygamy was destined
to be phased out as women became empowered and
the younger Sheikhs became modernized. After all,
Jan couldn't help but notice a recent spate of dash-
ing young Sheikhs marrying American women and
popping out babies like they were back in the Garden
of Eden. She needed to get some insight into this old
practice before it was gone and everyone was just in
boring, civilized one-on-one marriages!

But how to get one of these Sheikhs to talk openly about what was traditionally a very guarded part
of Arab culture? And even if she did get someone to
open up, how would she get to what she was really
after? The real question: Sex in a shared marriage.

Because that was what intrigued the world most
about any marriage that involved more than two people, right? People might not want to admit it, but it's

the first thing that anyone thinks about when they hear of a three or four or five person marriage: How does the sex work? Is there a schedule? A priority? Completely ad hoc? A goddamn orgy every night?! And if she could get some insight into that, it would be new. The research would be important, and it would also be interesting. Maybe a book deal. Real publicity. Not that Jan cared about fame that much, but becoming a celebrity professor with a popular book would certainly grease the skids when it came to tenure.

"Does my face look greasy?" she asked the mirror as she leaned forward and touched her plump cheek and pursed her lips. "Dammit. I thought the desert was a dry heat, so why am I so hot and sweaty?! It must be the humidity in this damn single-person restroom. I should get the hell out—"

She stopped mid-monologue as the dark wooden door to the supposedly locked restroom swung wide open and a tall tuxedo-clad Arabian man strode in like he owned the damned place—restroom, hotel, and perhaps even her. Without flinching he looked her up and down, his eyes flashing green and narrowing slightly as his gaze followed the curve of her breasts down past her strong hourglass shape, all the way through to her thick bare thighs that were a bit spread because she'd been leaning forward to check out her fat greasy face in the mirror.

"Ah, yes, excuse me," he drawled in a devilishly deep

voice, his gaze unwavering, a tingle emerging at the base of Jan's neck as she realized that holy mother of hell this man was slowly closing the door behind him. "I was looking for my fiancée."

Jan straightened up and put her legs together, adjusting her glasses while suddenly wishing she'd taken her mother's advice—all her mother's advice: wrinkle cream, contact lenses, Botox, fat-loss pills, ass-reduction surgery . . .

"Well, she's not here," Jan said hotly, her jaw clenching as she fought the urge to adjust her glasses again. She cocked her head and held her arms out wide. "See? No fiancée. Just me and you in a single-person restroom. Anything wrong with this picture?"

The man smiled, showing beautiful, gleaming white, perfectly aligned, picture-perfect teeth that seemed to say he was perfect so there could be nothing wrong with any picture that had him in it. She blinked and took a quick breath as she noticed the strong line of his jaw highlighted by the manicured, impeccably groomed stubble that looked soft and organized but somehow still wild. His lips were dark red and full, his nose naturally straight and sharp, his dark hair richer and more vibrant than the deep black tuxedo jacket that had clearly been tailored to fit the masculine V of his body.

"There is nothing wrong with this picture," he said, letting the door fall shut and standing tall, neither his smile nor his shameless gaze showing any signs of letting up. "Me and you, as you said. Though I believe the grammatically correct phrasing would be 'You and I.' Is English not your first language?"

Jan felt herself go bright red, and the tingle that had started at the base of her neck quickly developed into a full-on line of electricity that made her tighten her asscheeks so hard she worried she'd get a cramp and fall down near the toilet, clutching her ass and screaming for help. Then he'd have to massage her rump to save her life, and then . . . wait, no, stop, you moron! Talk like an adult!

"I'm an American professor with a PhD and almost thirty papers published in my name," she said fiercely, wondering why she was defending herself when he was clearly messing with her. "And tailored tuxedo or not, I think you need to worry about your manners before attempting to correct my grammar."

The man frowned, touching his chin and looking down at her from his height, which seemed towering in the small enclosed space. He was lean, but still heavily muscled, judging by the outline of his thick pectorals that pushed almost obscenely against the fitted cotton broadcloth of his startlingly white shirt. She should feel threatened, but she didn't. Uncomfortable, yes. But not uneasy. Oh God, was she actually . . . turned on?

The thought hit her just as the subtle aroma of

his cologne rose up around her, a deeply masculine musk of red sage and tobacco leaf, with hints of sandalwood and raw spice. She blinked hard and adjusted her glasses again, wondering if they would fog up in this humid space. Should she just take off those glasses and shake open her hair, like in those cheesy movies where the ugly girl suddenly becomes beautiful when her pigtails come loose? Should she smile coyly and explain that she was conducting a scientific experiment on how sex worked in shared relationships, that she'd love to interview him, that if he'd just take a seat and give her a moment to hoist her butt up beside the sink and cross her legs seductively, they could begin.

"What is wrong with my manners?" he said, breaking her out of the fantasy that had her half-laughing, half-fainting as it occurred to her that either it was in fact very humid in here or there was some other reason she felt wet between the legs. "I did say excuse me, did I not?"

"And then you walked in and closed the door behind you," said Jan, regaining her senses and crossing her arms under her breasts, pushing them up without thinking even as her nipples stiffened in approval. "Which isn't just bad manners, but is downright threatening."

The man's jaw went tight, his eyes narrowing. He took a step toward her, but she held her ground, wishing she hadn't when she took in his warm, manly scent again and realized that no, it wasn't the humidity that was making her panties feel damp.

"So you are feeling threatened, my American professor with a PhD and thirty published papers?" he said slowly, the words oozing out of him with an erotic smoothness that made her want to slap him one moment, let him have his way with her the next. "Threatened by my formidable Arab presence? My dark skin? My foreign accent? My black hair? My exotic, erotic—"

"OK, stop!" she said, pushing past him and pulling open the door. "Are you for real? You walk in here looking for your fiancée, and the next moment you're all up against me? Have you no shame? Seriously, you're not helping to offset any of the awful stereotypes about how Arab men interact with women! Disgusting!"

The man stayed calm at her outburst, and he maintained his unflinching, coolly confident demeanor. He watched her with those deep green eyes as she turned in the open doorway to snap at him one last time before heading out of there. But before she got another word out, he spoke.

"Thirty three," he said calmly, touching his chin again and tilting his head back, showing off the perfect structure of his high cheekbones as the soft yellow light highlighted his face like this was a goddamn studio that he'd designed to make him look like a Greek god. Great genes, she thought absentmindedly, hating herself for thinking it. His children would be beautiful, wouldn't they? Ohmygod, stop!

"What?" she said, frowning as she wondered why she was still here, pleased that she was still talking in complete sentences. "Thirty three what?"

"Thirty three papers. That is how many you have published under your name. I have read all of them. Some are a bit redundant, but I understand that you have to keep publishing papers to stay relevant in American academia, so you are forgiven." He smiled and took a step toward her again. "You are also forgiven for calling me disgusting, obscene, threatening, and an Arab stereotype. You are forgiven, because I can tell that you are intrigued by me, mystified by me . . . attracted to me too, I sense."

She stepped back into the restroom without realizing it as the door slowly swung shut behind her, almost smacking her on the butt as if to tell her she was an idiot and she should turn and run. "What the hell?" she muttered. "What is this? Who are you?"

"Sheikh Darius of the Kingdom of Noramaar," he said. "And I am the answer to your prayers, just like you are the answer to mine, Professor Johansen."

2

Jan blinked hard and tried to shake the impression that she was slipping into a dream of some sort. Perhaps he was hypnotizing her with those mesmerizing green eyes. She'd seen some hypnotist make people do weird stuff at a show in college once. Maybe she was already holding her left ear and hopping on one leg and she had no idea!

"What are you talking about?" she asked, frowning as she tried to remember why the Kingdom of Noramaar rang a bell. She couldn't place it right then, and besides, she'd never heard of Sheikh Darius. So what if he'd read her papers. Her name was on the list of attendees for this conference. Anyone could have looked her up. A compliment at best. Downright creepy at worst. Walk away, Jan.

"I am talking about your latest research, which you have been cautious about making public so far. I have only seen hints of it in your papers, but enough to get my attention," he said. "Your views on shared marriages, and how in small hunter-gatherer tribes these shared sexual relationships created bonds that tightened the group dynamic. The Arab world is the only major society where any semblance of shared marriages exist, and I believe you are here to further your research. So I would like to help you. An experiment, if you will. One that could save your career." He took a breath and his green eyes darkened for a flash before regaining that cool light of confidence, but this time with a hint of vulnerability that lasted only a second but was real enough that it caught Jan by surprise. "And one that could save my kingdom."

Jan felt her heat rise along with that tingle, and this time it wasn't arousal. Suddenly she yearned to learn more, that hint of buried emotion in his words tugging at her as if to say you need to follow this path. But better sense prevailed, and she took a breath and forced a stern smile. "Um, thanks for the concern over my career, but I'm doing just fine. And—"

"Are you? According to someone I know on the University of Pittsburgh's Tenure Committee, your case is going to be a tough sell. You have a PhD in Biology, but you have shunned the Biology Department in favor of what they believe is a sensationalist mix of popular pseudo-science and a dangerous hunger for celebrity status."

Jan would have fallen off her chair if she'd been sitting on one. As it was, she leaned back against the restroom door, doing her best not to sway as a dizzy spell came and then thankfully passed when she remembered to breathe. What the hell was some Sheikh doing talking to the University of Pittsburgh's Tenure Committee about her case?! And why in the hell would anyone on the committee say something to an outsider! He was lying. He was playing her. Why?

"You're lying," she said flatly. "Bullshit."

"A king does not lie," said the Sheikh, and she saw his chest muscles flex beneath that tuxedo jacket, like every fiber in his hard body was attesting to his statement. His eyes said it too. This man was serious. Serious about what? "I have donated four million dollars anonymously to Pitt over the past eighteen months." He smiled. "Of course, anonymous simply means my name will not be published anywhere. The university president and every tenured faculty member know who I am, and they are all very happy to grant me an audience when I seek it. Or a favor if I ask it."

Jan cocked her head and pushed her glasses back up her nose. She couldn't believe what she was hearing. It could be true, or it could still be bullshit. And if it were true, it was . . . it was . . . "Blackmail?" she snarled. "Are you threatening me? Threatening my career?"

The Sheikh smiled and took a breath. "I am a positive man, so I prefer to think of it as a bribe instead of a threat. I wish only the best for you, Professor Johansen. I admire your ideas, and I admire your . . ." He paused as he glanced down at her chest and then flinched as his breath caught. Jan felt her own body respond, but she did her best to keep that stern, I-hate-you look on her face.

I gotta get out of here, she thought as the mixed signals from her own body and mind threatened to take her down a path that felt dark and dangerous for a reason she couldn't understand. This is too weird. Just too damned weird.

"And I'd like to say I admire your shamelessness and sheer gall, but I don't," she said, pushing herself away from the threshold and stepping out into the cool air-conditioned hallway, immediately feeling a bit more composed. "Besides, if I recall correctly, you were looking for your fiancée, so I suggest you go find her."

He smiled and shook his head, touching his chin again and pulling gently at his thick stubble. Then his eyes locked in on hers. "You misunderstood me, Professor Johansen. Yes, I did say I was looking for my fiancée. But I have found her. She is you."

3

Sheikh Darius watched the curvy American professor walk away from him without saying another word. For a slow-moving moment he was mesmerized by the way her wide hips moved in that tight black skirt, and he had to force himself to blink and look away before his own pants got too tight around the crotch. Ya Allah, there was a magnetism to her that he did not expect. From the photographs he'd seen he knew she was pretty, with beautiful brown eyes and lustrous dark curls that complemented her creamy skin, whose tone hinted at a wonderful blend of American ethnicities. Yes, she was in her thirties, but Darius had played his games with the twenty-year-old supermodels of Europe and South America, and the artificial lips and sunken cheekbones did nothing for him anymore. Still, he was surprised at the attraction he'd felt. It excited him in more ways than just the obvious. Perhaps it even changed things.

"Perhaps I came on a bit too strong," he muttered to himself as he waited for Jan to turn the corner before he ambled towards the main conference room where he knew she was scheduled to give a presentation in an hour. "Too much, to the point where I cannot blame her for feeling suspicious at the least, threatened at the worst. I should not have brought up the fiancée thing. But what to do? What I propose cannot be approached in any simple way! Certainly the logical thing would have been to simply talk with her and explain everything up front. But this is not a business transaction. It is more. It needs emotion and upheaval, electricity and attraction. It cannot work if either of us is faking it. You cannot sit in a conference room and negotiate something like this. It has to be dramatic! So I was prepared to try anything to get her to listen: blackmail, bribery, seduction. Now that I have put my foot in it and scared her off, what option do I have left? I could attempt to reason with her again, but I can see in her eyes she is not one to bend to blackmail or reach for a bribe. As for seduction . . . ya Allah, I feel the attraction and it could work. But in a way, seduction would be the most dishonest way to pull her into this, would it not? If we make love and then I tell her my plan, she will feel manipulated, betrayed, used! So can it be that the most drastic option will actually be the most honest? Can I do it? Can I take her back to Noramaar against her will, create that upheaval in her life, generate those emotions that can fuel an attraction that will convince her to enter into this madness?"

"Talking to yourself again, Darius," came the mocking voice from his left, casual and deep, making the Sheikh's jaw go tight when he realized it was him: Sheikh Ephraim of Habeetha, the small but powerful kingdom across the Golden Oasis that divided their two nation-states. "Perhaps you are in fact the mad Sheikh, like they say."

Darius turned on his heel and stopped, looking directly into his eyes and holding the gaze until Ephraim blinked and casually looked past him to break the intense eye contact. "Who is they, Ephraim? The women of your harem, who, as I understand it, are the only people in your lawless kingdom who actually agree with anything you say. Certainly your Council of Ministers do not, if what I saw at the last Pan-Arabian Convention still holds. If I remember correctly, your entire Council voiced strong disagreement with your war-mongering rhetoric over the past three years."

Ephraim smiled and ran his fingers through his hair, which was long and wavy, almost down to his shoulders. He stood a few inches shorter than Darius, but was still taller than most men. He was also thick and broad: certainly as broad and muscular as any in his admittedly impressive army, which had been growing in size after Ephraim had made the controversial move of inviting fresh Islamic immigrants from the more oppressive regimes to become full citizens of Habeetha if they served in his military for five years. Full citizenship meant receiving a stipend from the oil and tourism revenues of Habeetha, and thousands—mostly young men—had flocked to take advantage of the young Sheikh's limited-time offer.

"Are you feeling threatened, Sheikh Darius?" Ephraim said, still smiling as he rubbed the heavy stubble on his chin and cheeks.

"No, but perhaps I should," Darius said, maintaining his calm but narrowing his eyes ever so slightly. "The neighboring Sheikh builds an army that is almost as large as his entire nation. He stations them along the banks of the Golden Oasis, whose fresh waters have been peacefully shared by Habeetha and Noramaar for centuries. Then he is rumored to be working on plans to dam up the underground aquifers that feed the Golden Oasis, drawing the fresh water out through pumps and wells, which would eventually lead to a catastrophic drop in the water levels of the oasis itself." Darius stopped for a moment, considering his next words. He expected to see Ephraim here, just like he'd expected to make his acquaintance with Professor Janice Johansen. He'd pushed it a bit too far with Jan already. Was he about to make the same mistake with Ephraim? In public he'd often responded to Ephraim's aggressive statements with equal bombast and challenge, but that was about politics and perception. In private he'd never crossed the line. "It would also lead to war," he said quietly, before he could stop himself.

Ephraim did not flinch, his smile widening in a way that made Darius wonder which of them better deserved the title of the mad Sheikh. This game they'd been playing over the past three years was mad enough. Real war would be insane!

"Rumors. Speculation. He said. She said. They. This. Them," said Ephraim through that smile. "In the end the only relevant word is Us. You and I. We are kings, and we decide. No one else matters. Now, what are you drinking, old friend?"

Darius took a breath and allowed himself to relax. Though Ephraim was younger, they'd both attended Oxford at the same time, two Muslim kings playing at being Brits at Magdalen College. They'd had their moments together, most notably the one night that Darius had been swayed by the members of the rugby team to try alcohol. He'd ended up drunk out of his mind on Irish whiskey, and in fact it was Ephraim, who was already an old hand with the bottle, who made sure the young Sheikh Darius made it back to his room in one piece. That was a long time ago, and to say they were friends was a stretch. But they were not exactly enemies either. Not yet, at least.

"Sweet tea, as always," said Darius.

Ephraim smiled and winked. "Of course. Do not worry. The secret of your indiscretion is safe with me. Now, shall we walk into the conference hall together, making tongues wag as the people wonder whether we will draw swords and face off against one another on the main stage?"

Darius laughed and walked ahead, holding the door

to the conference room open for Ephraim and inviting him to enter first. The entire hotel had been cleared of unauthorized guests for the conference, and security on the grounds was so tight that the Sheikhs and billionaires roamed freely in the hallways unburdened by their personal security details. It had added an almost casual atmosphere to the conference, and combined with the almost-western metropolitan vibe of Dubai, made the far reaches of the Arabian Peninsula seem like another world.

Do not get lulled into thinking this is not a very serious game, Darius reminded himself as he followed Ephraim into the gigantic room lined with rows of plush leather chairs facing a lavishly decorated stage on which a panel of Arab academics were politely debating whether it was hypocritical for the oil-rich Arab nations to move to solar energy while continuing to get rich selling oil to the West and the rest of Asia. Ephraim was charismatic and intelligent, greatly loved by the younger generations of Habeetha, admired by many in Noramaar as well. But he was also ambitious and unpredictable, with a hunger for the external symbols of wealth and power that held little interest to Darius.

Indeed, at Oxford, while Darius rode a bicycle because he enjoyed the simplicity, Ephraim roared through the narrow streets in a gold-plated Lamborghini Diablo, wore Seville Row suits that he discarded after a single use, and hosted parties so lavish that even the children of the British royals and Russian billionaires were shocked at the displays of opulence. In fact it was at one of those parties—when Darius had thankfully returned to drinking his sweet tea—that someone had passed a remark so cutting that Darius was certain Ephraim still bore the psychological scar.

"Oy, great King Ephraim," one of the drunk Brits, the obnoxious son of a minor Duke, had said. "Isn't your little nation of Habeetha smaller than the slums of Liverpool? And don't they say that the size of a king's nation is a smashing indicator of the size of his . . . cock?"

The roaring laughter had almost drowned out the last word, and although it should have been minor in the grand scheme of things drunk college students say, Darius, sober as always, remembered the dark cloud that crossed Ephraim's face at the time. That Duke's son had mysteriously been jumped and beaten senseless a week later outside a pub, and no one had ever taunted Ephraim after that. But Darius had noticed a change in Ephraim since that night. It was like a darkness had taken up residence somewhere inside the younger Sheikh after that public humiliation, planting a seed that had grown over the years.

And now Ephraim and his army looked out over the waters of the Golden Oasis, to the smooth dunes of Noramaar. Can one small seed sprout a tree so heavy and twisted? Who knew. What mattered is that's where they were in this game.

The thought reminded Darius why he was here, for whom he was here. He glanced over towards the left of the stage, a spark of electricity whipping through him when he saw her smooth curves as she sat there, one leg crossed over the other as she listened on headphones to the translators interpreting the Arabic words of the ongoing session.

"I will sit with the other attendees from Noramaar," Darius said. "But speaking of tongues wagging, I do recommend you listen to this next speaker. An American professor with some interesting ideas." He paused and bit his lip before narrowing his eyes at Ephraim. "Not so bad on the eyes either. Be sure to get a seat with a good view."

4

The view from the podium almost made her choke with nervousness. Jan had spent her career standing in front of groups and speaking with clarity and confidence, but this was different. It was mostly foreign, bearded men in the room, half of them putting on headphones because they didn't speak English, which meant they wouldn't be hearing her voice, her intonations, her cheesy one-liners and wise-ass phrasings. The other half were looking at their gold-plated iPhones, and the few men that were paying attention seemed more interested in her legs than the first slide of her presentation up on the big screen.

She took deep breaths and scanned over the crowd as she waited for the host to introduce her in Arabic and then in heavily accented English. The announcer was midway through her qualifications when Jan's gaze rested on a pair of blazing green eyes that made her heart jump.

Oh, God, it's him! Sheikh Darius, she thought as she swallowed hard and told herself so what. Pretty much everyone in the hotel was here for the conference. You had to know he'd be in here.

It was almost time for her to start when the thoughts of that unexpected encounter in the restroom came flooding back to her. Now as she stared into his eyes, she suddenly remembered why Noramaar sounded familiar. It was on the banks of the famous Golden Oasis, a massive body of fresh water almost as large as one of the Great Lakes. It was unique in that two kingdoms shared that one oasis: Noramaar and the kingdom of Habeetha, which had been in the news a few years ago for inviting a horde of new immigrants even though the livable land area seemed unable to handle it. The move had invited speculation of a future land-grab by the young, brash, long-haired Sheikh Ephraim, who was known as a renegade in that he'd allowed alcohol to be sold in his kingdom, legalized prostitution, and was openly tolerant of the banned practice of gambling. Habeetha was often called the Las Vegas of Arabia, and so it was no surprise that when Ephraim opened his borders for six months, young men from the more conservative nations of the Arabian Peninsula poured in, happily agreeing to serve five years in the army in return for a lifetime of a monthly stipend and citizenship in Sin City, Arabia!

A round of polite applause rose up as the host finished the introduction, and Jan heard herself start speaking. Years of habit and practice kicked in, and she breezed through her presentation in record time, even drawing a few laughs with her one-liners. The talk had been fairly innocuous—nothing about her racier theories of shared marriages and societies in which they flourished. This wasn't that kind of conference. She took a few questions and then walked off the stage to the secluded dressing area where she'd prepped earlier. There'd been a pot of tea there, but it had been replaced with an inviting looking glass of lemon-infused water.

"Congratulations on an exceedingly boring lecture, Professor Johansen," came his voice from behind her as Jan gulped down the tall glass of lemon-water. The tone was flirtatious and teasing. "How did you even get invited to this conference?"

She knew who it was before she even turned. By then she could smell his intoxicating musk, and once again it made her body wake up. Does he feel this magnetism, she wondered as she looked up and met his gaze, his green eyes dancing with spirit as if he was inviting her to get on the dancefloor with him, play whatever game he had in mind.

"I was the only American professor to apply, I believe," she said licking the tart lemon off her lips and smiling, even though she knew she was setting back feminism about fifty years by even engaging with an entitled chauvinist who'd invaded her space. "And maybe they thought I was a man, since I used Jan Johansen on the application form."

Darius grunted, frowning as he glanced at her mouth, then her nose. He pulled out a white silk handkerchief from his pocket, and without hesitation reached out and dabbed at her face, just above her lips.

Startled, Jan swiped his hand away and stared at him. "What the hell?" she barked, looking around to see if anyone else was there. They were alone, and she was about to curse at him and then storm off, but then she saw the dots of bright red on his white silk kerchief. "What the hell?" she said again, her head buzzing when she realized it was blood. Her blood. Just a speck, and when she touched her face again there was no more. But it was clearly her blood.

The Sheikh grimaced and looked at his watch, his calm demeanor revealing a crack in it, like he was angry, upset, perhaps at himself. He looked into her eyes again, his own eyes soft with emotion, perhaps an apology. "Ya Allah, it seems mad, but this was the best way. The most honest way. Come, Jan. Lean on me. I do not want you to fall and break your glasses. I am not sure we will have time to have a new pair made before we get to Noramaar, and I would like you to see the Golden Oasis from the plane before we land."

"What . . . the . . ." she gurgled when she felt her vision start to blur. The Sheikh came close and slid his arm around her waist just as she swooned and collapsed against his hard body. Through the haze she

saw that empty tumbler, her lipstick smudge looking red and vibrant against the shimmering glass.
She tried to say something again, but only gibberish came out. She looked into his eyes, a moment of
clarity coming over her as she clawed at his muscled
back while he held her firm. "Poison," she managed
to mutter, clenching her teeth and then absurdly trying to bite at his face as her thoughts slurred along
with her words.

"Do not be ridiculous," he whispered against her
hair, and there was that beautiful, intoxicating
smell of his body again. "Why would I poison the
woman I am planning to marry? It is so much more
Sheikh-worthy to simply drug and kidnap you, don't
you agree? Do not worry about the blood. In your
drink was *aruha*, a natural extract from a desert cac-
tus found in Noramaar. In high doses it can dry out
the nasal passages very quickly, sometimes causing
minor bleeding. Come now. Hold tight and relax.
My plane awaits. My head cleric is on board, and
your handmaidens are readying your wedding gown.
In five hours you will be my wife, and the queen of
Noramaar. After that I will explain everything, and
then you will have the option of backing out if you
so choose."

"Psycho," she managed to gurgle as she felt him
lead her deeper into the interior of the hotel, down
a heavily carpeted hallway, toward a white wooden

door, beyond which she thought she could see her own future—a future where she was screaming wildly while still clawing at his muscular back. "Help," she whispered weakly, wondering if she was walking or being carried, alive or in a dream-state on her way to the land of the dead. "Someone help. Psycho. You're a goddamn psycho."

"Perhaps," he said, kicking open the door and dragging her out into the blinding sunshine, where a black limousine was waiting, its back door wide open, two bearded guards standing watch. "But look at the bright side. You can call your mother and tell her you just married a king. Here. See."

She was sprawled haphazardly on the red leather backseat of the limousine, for some reason wondering why she wasn't unconscious yet if she'd been drugged. She watched in semi-disbelief as the Sheikh opened a blue jewelry box, out of which stared a diamond the size of her eyeball, perched atop a ring of shimmering gold.

And then, finally, she passed out, amidst a swirling mental image of piercing green eyes and shining gold.

5

When Jan awoke she was firmly seatbelted into a plush reclining chair by a window that was as big as her dining table back home—which wouldn't have been that remarkable if not for the fact that she was on an airplane. She blinked and looked down at her hands, wiggling her bare fingers and frowning because the last thing she remembered was being shown a wedding ring by the Arab serial killer who'd drugged and kidnapped her.

"I changed my mind," he said, as if to explain why the ring wasn't on her finger after all. She looked up and saw Darius calmly sitting across from her in a matching leather recliner, a steaming pot of tea on the smooth wooden table beside him. "My apologies for scaring you more than was necessary. The truth is, after meeting you in person, I have gotten turned around a bit. It is unusual. A bit troubling."

Jan took a breath and blinked away the haze. She felt relatively clear-headed even though she could feel a dull ache at the base of her neck. She glanced down at her ringless fingers again, then at her bare thighs, realizing she was still in her skirt-suit and not the wedding dress that her abductor's handmaidens were supposedly preparing for her.

"I'm not sure if I'm relieved or insulted," she said, surprised at her own remark, even more surprised at her involuntary smile. Just like the encounter in the restroom, although by all signs this guy was unhinged and dangerous, she just didn't get that creepy vibe from him. There was something about the way Darius carried himself that seemed supremely grounded, firmly centered, like he knew exactly what he was doing, like he was doing it for a reason that was gravely important. Of course, it didn't hurt that he was gorgeous, but they said Ted Bundy was good-looking too. Still, Jan trusted her instincts, and though this looked bad on paper, it felt disconcertingly OK to her gut.

"Why would you be insulted?" the Sheikh said with a frown, pouring two cups of the delicious-smelling spiced tea and placing one on her side-table.

"Because what does it say about me if a psycho kidnapper has a ring and wedding dress all set to go for his stolen bride and then says he's changed his mind? I don't know if that's better or worse than being stood up at the altar! My mom would disown me! Can't even get a serial-killer to go all the way, can you, Janice?" she said, taking a sip of the tea and shuddering at how the warm, sweet thickness of the milk made her feel. Suddenly she felt elated, and it hit her that maybe this desert-cactus extract did more than just knock you out. Jan hadn't messed with drugs much, but she did understand biology, and she could tell that her serotonin-receptors were firing in overdrive. This was clearly a happy-time drug, and it was working. No wonder she was cracking one-liners with an Arab monster who'd just kidnapped her. "Oh, God, that's good," she said after taking another deep sip of the sugary-sweet tea, the warm milk making her feel safe and almost giddy with joy. "Now, this is the drug you should've used on me."

The Sheikh's frown deepened, and he rubbed the stubble on his chin, glancing out the window for a moment before looking into her eyes. "You are not angry?"

"Oh, believe me, I'm angry," she said, sipping the tea again and crossing one leg over the other, not missing the way his eyes darted downwards before he quickly retrained them on her face. "But I've met my share of creepy dudes over the years. I don't want to speak too soon, since everything you've said and done so far says you are in fact a psycho creepshow, but you just don't give off that vibe. Don't get me wrong, what you just did was beyond acceptable, clearly illegal, and will neither be forgotten nor forgiven. But I'm a practical person, and it's clear that since I haven't been dismembered, murdered, or raped while I was passed out, those probably aren't your intentions."

She took another sip of the tea, licking her lips and sighing as she felt herself relax when she realized that what she just said actually did make a lot of sense. "Also, I think this cactus-drug has something to do with the fact that I'm angry but for some reason smiling my ass off."

The Sheikh raised an eyebrow and put on an innocent look. "Interesting. That would explain why the men and women who harvest the *aruha* are always in such a good mood, even though they are sunburnt beyond recognition and covered in cactus-spines after a day in the desert."

"Oh, please. You wanted to put me in this weird, uninhibited state of mind. You knew exactly what you were doing."

The Sheikh took a sip of his tea and shrugged. "I thought I did. Now I am not so sure."

Jan looked into his eyes, trying to figure out if it was the drug or if she was really seeing something in his look. "What do you mean?"

"I am not sure what I mean, Janice."

"OK, you can call me Jan now. I don't like Janice. Even my mother doesn't call me Janice."

"Really? Why would your mother not call you by your given name? Did she not name you?"

"We are not talking about my mother right now. Don't change the topic. You were about to apologize, I believe."

The Sheikh frowned again and shook his head. "No. I do not lie, and I do not apologize."

Jan laughed. "What else do you not do? Clearly, drugging and kidnapping someone is something that you do do!" She snickered like a schoolgirl. "Hee hee. I said doo-doo!"

The Sheikh tried to contain his smile. "I think perhaps we should have this conversation when you are sober, Professor Johansen."

"I think if I were sober, Sheikh Darius, the only conversation we'd be having is about which country's prison you'd be locked up in for what you just did. Maybe you could plead insanity and go to a psych ward for the rest of your days. Now, since you've got me in probably the best mood you're ever going to see me in, this is your only shot at convincing me you're not actually a psycho."

Darius stayed silent, his eyes searching her face like he was looking for something. Then he glanced out the window, gesturing with his head as he looked down. "There," he said softly. "The Golden Oasis. The waters of life. The only source of fresh water for almost five million people."

Jan leaned over and looked out, and the sight took her breath away. A perfect circle of shimmering water, stretching so wide it looked like an ocean. Palm trees and desert flora lined the banks like a protective ring, boundless dunes of golden sand stretching in all directions beyond. It looked like a dream. A fantasy. Make believe. Sorta like the situation she was in right now.

"It's gorgeous," she whispered. "I've seen pictures, but they don't do it justice."

"Yes," said the Sheikh. "Sometimes I too find that pictures do not do justice to the real thing."

Something in the way he said it made her glance back at him, and Jan's heart jumped when she saw how he was looking at her. Darius held the gaze for a long moment before suddenly turning away, as if he was afraid of what she'd see in his eyes. Too late, she thought. I already see it.

"Why am I here?" she asked, glancing at the Sheikh, then at the majestic oasis, finally back at him again. "What do you want from me? You've read my research. You mentioned shared marriages. You've threatened my career. Then you attempted to bribe me by saying you'll help my career. Finally you drugged me and kidnapped me, even though I could see in your eyes that it wounded you to do so. You clearly had some plan to force me into marriage, but you seem to have backed away from that. And all of this is on the first day. So help me out here. I may be drugged up, but none of this makes sense."

"My fear is that it will make even less sense once I explain," said the Sheikh. "Ya Allah, perhaps I am insane. Perhaps the best thing is to turn back, drop you off in Dubai, and apologize even though I do not generally apologize for my actions." He paused and clenched his jaw. "You know what, Jan? I am giving you that option right now. Say the word, and I deposit you back at your hotel in Dubai. I will provide you with any compensation you ask to make up for what I have put you through. I will distance myself from anything to do with your career, one way or the other, and you will never see me again. If you choose, the past ten hours can go down in history as a strange, unexplained adventure in your life. End of story. No explanation. Just an apology and a farewell."

Jan took a breath and narrowed her eyes. Was he still playing her or was he serious? She couldn't deny she was curious. A Sheikh follows her career, donates millions of dollars anonymously so he'd have leverage over her tenure in case he needed to either blackmail or bribe her in the future. Why her? She was still a relative nobody in her field. The only unique thing about her career was her latest theories on shared relationships and marriages, most of it only hinted at in public documents. Why such a deep interest?

She looked at him again. Had he always planned to give her this choice to back out before he told her everything? No, she decided. I don't think so. I think he's actually turned around a bit, like meeting me has messed up his plans, like he's feeling that attraction too—an attraction that wasn't part of the plan. And least not yet.

"Before I passed out," she said, "you said something about how this was the most honest way. Which means you need to be honest first, and then I get to decide whether I want to go back to Dubai or not. You can't force me to choose before I've heard the full story."

The Sheikh thought for a moment. "The full story cannot be written without your help, Jan. And I was uncertain how to best secure your cooperation. I was prepared to try blackmail, bribery, coercion, kidnapping. The stakes are high enough that I was prepared to do anything to get you on board."

"Pretty extreme, don't you think? Why not just talk to me? That would have been a nice middle-ground between blackmail and kidnapping."

Darius grinned. "Of course. Why did I not think of that." Then he sighed. "Jan, if my predicament could be solved by words, we would not be here. The idea is so extreme that talking about it before I had some leverage over you would be pointless. You would either laugh at me or call me insane."

"Seems pretty close to where we're at now, I'd say," she retorted. "Go on."

"The other option was, of course, seduction," he said, sipping his tea and meeting her gaze in a way that made her gasp.

"Excuse me?"

He ignored her surprise. "But that would have been dishonest. To get involved with you before you knew my motives would be wrong."

"I think we're getting a bit presumptuous here," Jan said, still a bit shaken but trying her best to look indignant. "But go on. What are your motives?"

"It took me years to steady my resolve to follow this path. It is unprecedented, perhaps insane. But then once I decided to do it, I had to hedge my bets. I had to make sure I could turn to any method, based on your reaction." He sighed again. "Of course, it was my own reaction that sent things down this admittedly extreme path. My reaction when I came face to face with you and felt the pull of an attraction so intense it scared me. That is when I knew that if I spent time with you, just talking, getting to know you, it would lead to . . . to . . ."

"To what?" Jan said, her breath catching as her heart raced to finish his sentence. "Lead to what?"

"Bloody hell there is no use," he muttered, gritting his teeth. "I cannot fight it. Even though I know where this will lead."

"What, Darius?" she said again, every fiber in her body tingling with electricity as the sun reflected off the waters of the Golden Oasis, casting both of them in shimmering golden light, the air around them sparkling, shining, glistening, gleaming. "Lead to what?"

"Lead to this," he growled, and then he was on her, his lips pushing against hers, his hard body crushing hers into the plush seat, the teacups flying off the tables, their combined heat rising so fast she cried out in shock.

"Oh, God," she moaned as her head spun and her body thrashed and the heat roared through her body with a force that shattered her will to resist. "Oh, God, Darius."

He pulled back for a moment, looking into her flushed face as if searching for some indication that she wanted him to stop. But there was none, just her eyes looking into his, her body moving against his. So he leaned in again and he kissed her. By God, he kissed her.

6

The Sheikh wanted to pull away but the only pull was the force of attraction taking him deeper into her, deeper into this madness. His mind swirled as he pushed his tongue into her warm mouth, his fingers undoing her seatbelt and pulling her jacket open, his hands closing on her breasts as she moaned and gurgled into his mouth.

"Oh, God," she moaned as he pinched her nipples so hard he felt her back arch, pushing her chest forward. "What are you doing? What are you doing to me?"

"I will stop if you say it," he muttered, pulling away from her and looking into her eyes. Would it matter if she said yes or no? Would he be able to stop? Was the drug still strong in her system? Was this already rape, no matter what she said? Ya Allah, he was no better than Ephraim, was he?! "Say no and I stop," he muttered again even as he felt her nipples stiffen beneath her white satin blouse, the twin peaks hard and pointy like arrowheads between his thumbs and fingers.

"You wouldn't be much of an evil Sheikh if you

took the trouble to drug and kidnap me and then wimped out when it came to raping me," she said, and the statement shocked him even as it gave him an erection so strong he almost passed out as the blood rushed from his head to meet the demands of his swollen cock.

Now he knew he wasn't stopping, and with a roar he stood and pulled Jan off the seat, dragging her down the carpeted aisle of the plane and tossing her face-first into an overstuffed day-bed that stretched across the back of the plane. She screamed as he smacked her ass three times with all his strength, pushed up her skirt, and ripped her panties off, tearing them down the middle. He brought her panties to his face, sniffed deep of her scent, almost passing out again when he felt his balls tighten from the realization that she was wet for him, hot for him, ready for him.

He held her torn panties in his mouth, growling as he undid his heavy belt with his left hand, holding her face-down ass-up with his strong right arm. Her smooth round buttocks were turning an intense red from his hard slaps, and she was moaning and gasping from the shock of what had just happened.

The Sheikh's cock sprang out as he pushed his trousers and underwear down, and he roared when he felt his erection lead him to the dark space between her open thighs. He could see the matted brown curls of her sex from behind and beneath, and her aroma was all he could smell, taste, see, feel. He wanted her. He needed her. And he was going to take her.

Darius grabbed her hair and yanked her head back as he pressed his cock against her soft naked ass, taking the wet panties he'd been biting on and shoving them into her mouth. Then, still holding her hair tight by the roots, he pulled back and ran his hand down along her rear crack, spreading her from below with his strong fingers, rubbing her slit to make sure she was wet enough.

He growled again when he felt her dripping onto his fingers, and he lined up the angry head of his throbbing cock with her damp entrance, his entire body seizing up at the first sensation of her heat, the way her delicate hairs teased his swollen shaft as he rubbed back and forth, opening her up.

"Drugged, kidnapped, and raped," he whispered in her ear as he pushed a few inches into her and held his cock there as he felt her cunt slowly open up. He dug his fingers into her hair again as she thrashed and snorted, her whimpers and wails sounding muffled from the panties stuffed in her mouth. He pulled back for a moment, and then drove his hips forward with a steady, raw power that took his heavy shaft so deep into her he swore he could feel parts of her vagina opening up as if for the first time. "And you know what? I am not even the evil Sheikh in this story."

7

A hundred miles away, Sheikh Ephraim watched his semen spurt all over the naked brown buttocks of the woman spread before him on the red, hand-woven Persian rugs that covered the sandstone floors of the southern wing of Habeetha's Royal Palace. He glanced down at the petite hand of the second woman who was furiously jerking him off, her fingers looking tiny wrapped around his thick shaft. Ephraim knew he was coming, but it felt like nothing. He grunted as he pulled the woman's hand away from his cock, turning away from the naked nubiles and walking towards the back balcony that overlooked a date-palm orchard. He stood there naked and bronze, the sunlight bearing down fiercely on him. Once again he looked at his cock, long and gleaming, thick and oozing. Then he snapped his fingers and gestured for the two women to leave.

He watched their bare bottoms move as they hurriedly gathered their robes. Once upon a time he would spend hours talking to the women of his harem, getting to know them, enjoying their spirited company and varied conversation before even touching them. He'd always enjoyed the challenge of making the women of his harem orgasm under his touch—it seemed like that was the ultimate test of a man's skills. Can you make a whore come every time?

Of course, the women of his harem were not prostitutes. They were not whores. They were not paid directly for their services, and they were free to leave at any time. What they got were private chambers in the southern wing of Habeetha's Royal Palace, every need taken care of—and Ephraim had always prided himself on making sure his company was their number one need. The women of his harem were his friends and confidantes, his lovers and his playmates. He used to know the hopes and fears of every one of his women. Now he barely even remembered their names.

That feeling of desolation returned to him as he stared out over the tops of the palm trees. The emptiness inside had been growing over the past few years, leading him to make decisions that he still wondered about. He'd angered every Sheikh and ruler in the region by violating Islamic law and allowing alcohol, prostitution, and gambling in Habeetha. But he'd had the last laugh when tourism skyrocketed, and within a few years Habeetha became known as a playground for young Arabs, the Las Vegas of Arabia, Sin City on the banks of the Golden Oasis! The new revenues were astronomical, and Ephraim knew that it would serve his country well in the long run, when oil was no longer the fuel of choice. Habeetha was oil-rich, but poor in other natural resources. If the oil money dried up, it would be a disaster. This way there was a second revenue stream.

Yes, he thought as he took a deep breath and squinted past the swaying treetops, towards the distant horizon. Tradition be damned. People gamble, drink, and fuck anyway. Better to have it accepted and regulated than hidden in shame and shadows. That was not a bad decision, not matter what the clerics and traditionalists said. But the other big move—opening up the borders and taking in thousands of young Arabs, providing them with money, alcohol, and sex while putting them in the military—ya Allah, that had set something in motion. Something big, dangerous, and irreversible.

He'd done it on a whim, overruling his own council by insisting that Habeetha would be able to handle the influx of immigrants. It had felt like a benevolent, expansive move: After all, if he was going to make Habeetha an oasis of openness, should he not also open the borders?

What Ephraim had not counted on was the lopsided gender mix of the immigrants. He'd expected there to be more men who chose to come, but not such an overwhelming majority that he was forced to close his borders after only six months. Ephraim had always liked the idea of required military service as part of a citizen's education, a way to combat laziness and sloth and build good physical health and mental habits. And he'd hoped that having a number of women doing military service would add something positive to his image as a modern Sheikh. But the vision of a large, modern army with a good-sized mix of women did not come to be. Instead he had a hundred-thousand young men living and training on the banks of the Golden Oasis, everyone wondering what came next.

Fantasies of a glorious war and conquest of new lands had played themselves out in the Sheikh's rich imagination countless times over the years, dating back to when he was a hot-blooded young student. A part of him still believed that a king's job was to expand his kingdom. Was that not what every great king throughout history, everywhere in the world did? Why do we remember Alexander the Great or Xerxes the Magnificent or Genghis the Khan? Because they were never satisfied with what they had. They always wanted more. They wanted it all.

Invading Noramaar would be unprecedented, but it might work. No doubt every Sheikhdom in the region would denounce it, but most of the neighboring kingdoms were too small to maintain large standing armies, and so their denouncements would be just words. Saudi Arabia was the only concern, but chances were they'd stay out of it as well. After all, Saudi Arabia and the United States were close allies, and the U.S. had no interest in getting involved in another Middle-Eastern war—especially one between tiny kingdoms like Noramaar and Habeetha. Which meant that the U.S. might well advise the Saudis to stay away and let the local Arabs fight it out for some land in the middle of the goddamn desert.

Dreams of conquest aside, Ephraim took no particular joy in sending men and women to their deaths. But the problem of overpopulation was real, after that rash move to open the borders. Habeetha was small, and most of its land was shifting sand and almost impossible to build towns and cities on. All the population lived in Habeetha's capital, on the banks of the Golden Oasis. And as the population grew, the only place to expand would be across those shimmering waters. To Noramaar, the land of Sheikh Darius. Ephraim had boxed himself in with his own actions. He could not simply kick out hundreds of thousands of immigrants! And when those immigrants had children and those children had more children, eventually Habeetha would be bursting at the seams! There was no longer a choice but to look to Noramaar!

Early on in the game Ephraim had decided that if he could provoke Darius into attacking Habeetha first, he might be able to get away with a quick and decisive response that would yield results while the rest of the Arab world bickered about who was the good Sheikh and who was the evil invader. So Ephraim had planted a rumor that he was secretly planning to dam up the underground aquifers that fed the Golden Oasis. Technically Ephraim had the right to do that—after all, it was his land. Darius had taken the bait, and now, three years later, the two Sheikhs were regularly trading veiled threats of aggression in speeches and local television appearances. Ephraim knew that Darius was the calmer, more level-headed of the two. But he also knew that Darius was supremely proud and fiercely competitive in his own way, and he'd hoped that Darius would lose his cool and perhaps send in some spies to investigate the rumors. Then Ephraim would capture the spies, publicly blame Darius for something nefarious like trying to assassinate him, and boom, justification for war!

But three years later it was all still talk. And that last meeting with Darius in Dubai made it clear that Darius was not going to lose his cool. He was content to play the game of words in the public arena. Darius was good at that. He understood that eighty percent of war is propaganda and publicity, and would keep doing battle in the press as long as possible.

The public eye is the battleground Darius has chosen and I must change that battleground to one where I have an advantage, Ephraim thought as he strolled back to his chambers and reached for his black silk robe. He draped the cool cloth over his broad, muscular frame, leaving it open in front, not caring that his long cock was hanging out obscenely when he summoned his female attendant to bring him some wine.

As he watched the veiled woman pour the thick red wine into a silver tumbler, something jogged Ephraim's memory about that meeting with Darius. Something Darius had said right before that American professor's lecture:

Not so bad on the eyes, Ephraim. Make sure you get a seat with a good view.

"Take the wine away and bring me some sweet tea," commanded Ephraim suddenly, his hand going to his face as he rubbed his jaw furiously. The remark was made in passing, but it was an odd statement coming from the "good Sheikh Darius," was it not? And the look on Darius's face when he said it . . . Ephraim had seen that look before, had he not? Years ago, when they were two Muslim kings at Oxford University in England. That one night when Darius had decided he would try alcohol, because, as he'd proclaimed at the time, a king must experience everything at least once.

A king must experience everything at least once.

And alcohol was not the only thing the two kings had experienced that one wild night. Experienced together.

"Ya Allah, Darius," Ephraim muttered as the attendant came back in with a pot of steaming tea and set it down, her dark eyes flashing as she glanced at his cock, which had hardened on its own in the few minutes she'd been gone. "Are you saying we should move our fight to a new battlefield?" He thought back to the curvy, dark haired American professor who'd taken to the stage in her skirt suit and confidently lectured to Sheikhs and billionaires, even drawing a few laughs. Ephraim had indeed gotten a good look at her: She was pretty, with wise eyes that were unfortunately mostly hidden behind those ugly glasses. Her curves were strong and compelling, with womanly hips and sturdy thighs that made him want to see what was beneath that tight black skirt of hers. Yes, there was something to her. "Still," he muttered as he sipped the tea and winced, wondering if the sweetness of Darius's favorite drink had driven the good Sheikh mad. "What sense does it make? How can that solve anything? How can she solve anything?"

Ephraim drained the tea and tossed the silver cup onto the teakwood table, striding to the balcony and staring out toward the distant shores of Noramaar across the oasis. Darius could play the game as well as anyone, Ephraim knew. He had something in mind with this woman. He was bringing her into the game. But why? Was he trying to signal that perhaps this could be resolved without bloodshed and without either Sheikh losing face by standing down? Was he not just changing the battlefield but changing the game itself?

"So what is my move now?" Ephraim muttered as he turned and went to his massive teakwood desk and flipped on the forty-inch retina computer display as he took a seat at the keyboard and quickly typed in the woman's name, frowning as the search results came back. "What is my move?"

8

Jan couldn't have moved if she wanted, the Sheikh's hold on her was so firm. She was completely immobilized, spread face-down on the soft mattress that seemed to occupy the entire width of the plane. His fist was coiled in her thick brown hair, down near the roots at the base of her neck. With his other hand he'd stuffed her own torn panties almost down her goddamn throat, ramming his beast of a cock into her from behind after spreading the lips of her vagina with his fingers.

She'd felt her own wetness drip down onto his hands as he teased her slit before entering, and although she could have spat out her panties and screamed for him to stop, she didn't. She couldn't. She wouldn't.

"You wouldn't be much of an evil Sheikh if you drugged and kidnapped me and then wimped out when it came to raping me," she'd said when he offered to back off.

Oh, my God, who was that woman who said that? Where did those words come from? Did I actually challenge this stranger, this man who's twice my size, a king in his own territory, a man who's abducted me and is basically above the law right now? Did I goad him into doing what he's doing? Am I a slut? A whore? A damaged, sick, twisted creature who deserves to rot in hell?

She heard her own muffled moans as he fucked her from behind, his powerful hips drawing back and pushing in with a force that sent ripples through her body each time he re-entered. Jan was so wet she thought she might have peed herself, but the aroma was pure sex, pure heat, pure madness.

"Oh, God," she mumbled through her gag as she smelled his naked body behind her, felt his left hand rest on her ass, strong fingers digging into her soft flesh, his right hand still firmly gripping her hair. "Oh, God, yes."

Yes, she thought again. I'm saying yes even though I know I might still be feeling the effects of that drug, that my judgment might be compromised, my instincts dulled. Just because I'm allowing him to rape me doesn't mean it isn't rape. It's still rape.

But then again her words came back to her, and she smiled as she heard Darius grunt and begin to seize up behind her, his thrusts becoming erratic as his grunts grew louder. Jan could feel her own orgasm building in her depths even as she felt his heavy balls slapping against her skin as he pumped her like a goddamn animal. Now she understood the mad arousal they were both feeling. Somehow the professor in her was still observing herself, even as the woman in her was moaning and shuddering as that orgasm drew closer like a killer in the night.

There's a reason the rape fantasy is still alive in today's women, she thought as she felt the first wave of her climax hit. Along with the open sexual relationships of our past, there's no denying that men took what they wanted back then, hard and fast, with force and power. The history of humankind is written in violence and rape, and those genetic memories are buried in our subconscious, coming alive only in the most private of moments. No woman wants to be raped. But the thrill of the fantasy still lives in the darkness of the feminine mind.

This man awakened that in me, she thought as her climax began to escalate and her head began to spin. Perhaps this entire charade of the kidnapping and the psycho behavior was part of his act to awaken those dark emotions of fear, emotions that are feeding my lust, feeding his need, making me wet, making him hard. But at the bottom of it all, I must feel safe with him, mustn't I? Otherwise there's no way I'd be . . . I'd be . . . I'd be—oh, God, I'm coming!

Now the full force of her climax hit, and Jan spat her panties from her mouth and let out a scream as she felt the Sheikh ram himself in one last time and then explode deep inside her.

"Ya Allah!" he roared, pouring himself into her as Jan's orgasm hit her so hard she almost passed out.

She felt the blast of his semen like a jet against the far walls of her vagina, and she gasped and drooled as she shuddered through her own climax. She was so stretched, so filled, so wet, so wild that the professor in her had long since given up analyzing and observing. It was only when she felt the Sheikh's viselike grip on her hair slowly loosen as he pumped the last of his semen into her depths that she felt her senses slowly crawl back into her.

"Oh, God," she muttered as she lay flat on her stomach, the Sheikh collapsing on top of her, his weight feeling wonderful, warm, even familiar. "What did we just do?"

"Kthyr jiddaan," he muttered into her knotted hair as he petted her head and kissed her cheek. "We did what was not supposed to happen until later. But now it has happened, and the game has changed. God help us all."

"All?" Jan whispered, frowning and smiling at the same time as she turned her head and received a warm kiss on her open lips. "There's just the two of us here, Darius."

"Not for long," the Sheikh said softly. He rolled off her and turned her body so she lay on her side, facing him. Again she saw that look in his eye, that combination of grave seriousness and deep conflict, that look of determination mixed with an undercurrent of vulnerability. "But none of this can work unless it is genuine, unless it is real, unless you are willing to consider what comes next. Unless you are willing to experiment, to experience."

9

The Sheikh watched her as she pushed her glasses up on her nose and kicked off her shoes, smiling wide as she dipped her bare toes into the clean waters of the Golden Oasis.

"Ohmygod, did I just contaminate the entire water supply for two kingdoms?" she said, giggling like a child as she pulled her foot out and turned to the Sheikh. "Talk about putting my foot in it!"

"Your one-liners are improving," Darius said, grinning as he kicked off his own shoes and stepped onto the sandy bank of the ancient oasis. "Does that mean you are completely sober now?"

"I don't think I'll ever be sober again," Jan muttered, her face going flush as the Sheikh took her arm and led her into the comfortably cool waters of the oasis. They stopped knee-deep in, the surface of the water just about kissing the hem of her skirt. "My God, this is surreal. I've never seen anything like it before. The oasis really is golden!"

"Refraction of light," said the Sheikh matter-of-factly, trying to ignore the sensation he got from holding her bare arm, feeling her energy so close to him. Yes, already he could tell that things had changed for him. This would be more difficult than he thought. Perhaps impossible.

"Oh, so you're a scientist now," she said, teasing him with her big brown eyes as she bent down and cupped her hand, bringing some of the water to her lips and taking a sip. "Hmm. That's good. Kind of a sweet, earthy taste."

The Sheikh shook his head. "Ya Allah, you are bolder than I. You do understand that we filter the water before drinking it."

Jan shrugged. "In the last twenty-four hours I've survived being drugged, kidnapped, and raped. I think I can handle botulism."

Darius laughed and grabbed her around the waist, pulling her into him and kissing her hard on the lips. He felt her glasses cut into his nose, and he backed away and pulled them off her, tossing them far into the oasis, a tiny splash signifying the end of them.

"I can't believe you just did that!" she shouted, pulling away from him and beginning to wade deeper into the waters. "That's the only pair I have, you asshole!"

The Sheikh watched her flounder around aimlessly, nowhere near where the glasses had gone under. Then he went after her and grabbed her just before she stepped off the hidden underwater ledge that would have plummeted her into deeper waters.

"Careful, my blind professor. These waters have their secrets," he whispered as he yanked her back and led her back to safety. "Come. It is time to head back to the Royal Palace. We have much to discuss."

Jan's expression changed, and she nodded as she held onto him and stepped back onto the bank. One glance into his eyes, and then she squinted and shook her head as if in disbelief. Was it disbelief at him or herself? Perhaps both. In a way the Sheikh was in a state of disbelief himself: After all, he'd told her his plan, given her back her phone, passport, and credit cards, and said she could walk away and he would accept the consequences of what he'd done to her. But yet she was still here.

She was still here.

10

Why am I still here, she'd asked herself a thousand times when Darius had finished explaining what he'd been planning.

"Neither Ephraim nor I can back down, not after three years of public posturing. And the problem of Habeetha's overpopulation is real and drastic. It might have been caused by Ephraim's haste and short-sightedness, but now it is also my problem to deal with. On the other side of Habeetha is uninhabitable desert and then the salty ocean waters of the Gulf of Oman. When the capital city can no longer hold the population, they will look to the borders of Noramaar."

"So open your borders to immigration," Jan had said as she listened to him talk, already understanding that Darius was perhaps as proud and immovable as he accused Ephraim of being. "If the options are invasion or immigration, then it's a no-brainer, right?"

The Sheikh had taken a breath, and Jan saw a cloud pass across his handsome face. "That would mean I am yielding to Ephraim's threats, Jan. It would mean that anyone can come to my borders, puff out their chest and threaten war, and I will bow my head and compromise." He'd shaken his head fiercely, his green eyes ablaze. "I know what you are thinking: that it is my stupid pride. But it is more than that. A king is a symbol to his people. You Americans have your flag and your troops, Hollywood and Wall Street, the Grand Canyon and the Rocky Mountains, Disneyland and Las Vegas. You have a vast source of achievements and culture from which your people draw pride and self-confidence. But my people have only their Sheikh. Only me, Jan. I do not bow to pressure. I will not bow to Ephraim and simply back down. It would lower me in the eyes of my people, while it would make Ephraim look stronger, more powerful. Perception matters in politics, Jan. If I simply yield and—"

"You could make him pay," Jan had said. "Let him continue to pay the stipend to the folks who move from Habeetha to Noramaar. Then it'll look like you're doing them a favor."

"A good idea, but then there is the issue of who decides which people actually move. Ephraim might want to ship the worst of his people—criminals and madmen perhaps! And it is my people who will need to adjust to the influx, live side by side with them! It is a complex, sensitive matter, with implications that will play out over generations. It is quite possible that even if I ignore my pride and open my borders now, in twenty years there will be war anyway! I know Ephraim. He has never been satisfied with his tiny kingdom. Every time he looks out across the Golden Oasis from his Royal Palace, he thinks of expansion, conquest, invasion. It is not personal. He and I do not hate each other. In fact I understand those dreams of conquest, because as a king I too have fantasies of ruling the world. But those days where kings ride out with armies to invade and plunder are long gone, and I have enough self-control to not let the fantasies lead me down the path of madness."

"So what's the solution then? Just fight it out?"

The Sheikh had given her a strange look. "In a way. But on a different battleground."

"And what's the battleground?" she'd asked, frowning at the way Darius was looking at her.

"Not what, but who," the Sheikh had said, his gaze unwavering, that look of seriousness returning, but this time mixed with a hint of darkness that made her shiver.

"What do you mean?"

"I mean you, Jan," he'd said. "You are the battleground."

And then she'd listened as the world began to spin away from any semblance of sense or sanity. She listened as the Sheikh told her that the only solution that made sense was a full integration of Noramaar and Habeetha. A merger. A union.

A marriage.

"We combine the kingdoms. Yes, there would be a million administrative details to take care of, but our councils and ministers would handle that if the decision were made," the Sheikh had said as Jan listened with wide eyes and a throbbing head as the pieces slowly fitted together like a jigsaw. A jigsaw in which she was that last piece, the one that held it all together. "The problem is, the biggest decision is one that can never be agreed upon: Who would be supreme Sheikh of the new union?"

Jan had nodded absentmindedly as the plane began to descend towards the black runway that stretched through the golden desert like a racing stripe. She understood that although the pride and arrogance of two kings was certainly at play here, it was more than that. Perception indeed mattered. The self-image of a kingdom is indeed founded upon the perceived strength and power of its king.

Or its queen.

"It is the only way," the Sheikh had said, his voice deep and low as he said it. "The only way Ephraim and I can ever combine our nations without losing face is if neither of us is supreme ruler of the new kingdom. We are both unmarried with no heirs or siblings. The idea is unprecedented, perhaps insane. But it could work. It could work well enough to save thousands of lives, create a stronger, bigger kingdom, preserve the peaceful sharing of the waters of the Golden Oasis for another hundred years."

"What are you saying?" she'd whispered as the plane swooped in for landing, that funny feeling in her gut almost making her pass out. "Darius, are you asking me to . . . to . . . what are you saying?!"

"Marry us," he whispered, his jaw set tight but his deep voice trembling at its core, his green eyes burning deadly serious, that hint of darkness still alive in them. "Marry us both, and become queen of the new land. One kingdom, one people, one union, one queen. And one marriage. Three ways."

11

"There's no way," she'd said when they got into a silver Range Rover and headed from the Royal Airport directly for the banks of the Golden Oasis. "There's no way you're serious. This is part of some weird act of yours. Just like the kidnapping. There's no way . . . I mean . . . God, I can't even . . ."

"You have questions, I presume," he'd asked, regaining his composure and putting on a pair of Porsche Design sunglasses as the smooth Range Rover pulled off the pebbled highway and onto the open sand without missing a beat.

"Questions? Um, why, yes, I do have questions!" she'd replied through a jaw that was clenched so tight she could already feel the headache coming in. "Setting aside the issue of how ridiculous this scheme is, the biggest question is why me? Of all the people in the world, why me? You don't know me. Ephraim doesn't know me. I'm not Arab, not even Middle Eastern!" She sucked in a breath and shook her head. "Also, I'm not insane."

The Sheikh had taken a breath and lowered his

sunglasses as he glanced down at her. "Everything you said is true except the last bit."

She laughed and shook her head, crossing her arms beneath her breasts and turning away from him, staring out at the sand dunes whipping by like golden waves. "I must be insane if I'm still here," she muttered.

"Exactly, Jan. I could have had this conversation with you in Dubai, in a conference room or at a dinner table. But instead I barged in on you in the restroom, saying things that were alarming at best, terrifying at worst. Then I drugged and kidnapped you. And then I . . . I mean we . . . I mean, Jan, you understand why I chose to start all of this in the most extreme, extraordinary, dramatic way I could think of, yes? I had to break us out of the ordinary world, take us into a world of madness and chaos, where the ridiculous is real, the nonsensical is normal." His voice softened, and it sent a tremble through her, making her think of that mad, chaotic, nonsensical encounter on the plane. "That is the world in which true attraction lives. True arousal. You know it. You felt it. And you reached for it, just like I did. True attraction, which is the only way this can work."

She'd taken a breath and slowly turned back to him. She thought for a moment, remembering the wild attraction that had consumed her on the plane, remembering what she'd said to him when he'd offered to stop, remembering the way he'd gone so damned hard and lost control when she'd said it even as she got wetter and hotter than she'd thought possible. "Yes," she said, trying her best to act like a cool-headed professor with a goddamn PhD. "I've studied the psychology of sexual attraction. And I do understand that attraction can't be a negotiation. It's not about logic and clear thought. It has to be felt. That's the reason we use the word arousal. It has to be awakened. Brought out. Torn out if need be." She blinked three times, not sure if she could look into his eyes. "You believe this would only work if the attraction is real. Real attraction." She'd made herself look at him then, and it had sent a tingle down through the seam of her body, making her buttocks tighten, her thighs clench, the hairs on her neck bristle as the world began to spin again. "Real attraction between you and me." Another breath as she allowed herself to think of what he was asking. "And real attraction between me and him. Sheikh Ephraim. A man I've never met. A man who you yourself said was the evil Sheikh in this story."

Darius had put his sunglasses back on, and Jan could tell it was so she wouldn't see the surprise in his eyes. Surprise, but also admiration. And something else. A look that told her so much. A look that said he already felt possessive over her, and that it wouldn't be easy for him even if she did agree to proceed.

But how to even proceed? What was next?

She'd stayed quiet as the car pulled up and stopped beneath the shade of a cluster of majestic date-palms, just steps away from the serene waters of the Golden Oasis. And when she stepped out of the car and glanced over the massive oasis, Jan understood why he'd brought her directly here even as he laid out his proposition. There was an energy to these waters. A surreal, magical flow to the air around it. She felt it. It was old, palpable, real. There was something both disturbing and tranquil about this place, like this oasis was a fulcrum, a point of balance, something upon which great forces of mystery and wonder rested in harmony. But a harmony that was delicate, that could unleash something dark if disturbed. Jan wasn't a particularly spiritual person, but something about this place was calling out to her. A feeling of being drawn here. Attracted. Awoken. Aroused?

So she'd stopped asking questions and just kicked off her shoes and stepped into the waters, feeling its energy enter her the moment she committed to walking in. She'd felt a strange familiarity when the Sheikh stepped in beside her, even though her common sense reminded her she'd known the man less than a day. Of course, none of the day's events had been common by any stretch, and so she dismissed common sense and played in those shimmering waters, laughing like a child, giggling like a fool, splashing and stomping, wading and stumbling.

"Those are my only pair, you asshole!" she screamed

when the Sheikh tossed her glasses away and kissed her like they were old lovers. But somehow she knew she wouldn't be needing them again. Those were glasses made for Professor Janice Johansen, and they'd served their purpose by seeing her this far, by allowing her to see this far. Now it was time to change her perspective, to try and see things differently, to try and see everything differently. Her next set of glasses wouldn't be black frames with plastic lenses. The next set would be glasses fit for a queen. Would they let her see even farther? Or would they blind her?

Suddenly she knew she'd already made the decision to move forward, that perhaps everything in her life had been preparing her for this. Preparing her for him. Preparing her for . . . them? Oh, God, how could she even consider this?!

"It has to be you, Jan," the Sheikh said as he led her out of the oasis and towards the Range Rover, where two veiled attendants were waiting with gold-embroidered towels monogrammed with Arabic letters. "Because you understand that shared marriages are part of humankind's history. You will be able to explain it to the world. Your entire career has been about explaining complicated things to an audience. You have the poise and confidence, the intelligence and the presence."

"I don't speak a word of Arabic," she said weakly,

protesting even though she could feel herself fill with a terrible excitement as she sat on the sideboard of the silver car and watched an attendant dab-dry her feet. "Wouldn't it make more sense to find an Arab woman? There's no shortage of articulate, educated Arab women these days, yeah?"

"What I am proposing would be shocking even to the Arab world, where shared marriages are only the other way around, with one man taking multiple wives. Bringing an Arab woman into this would make the entire thing about religion and tradition. This is beyond that. Bigger than that. It needs to go beyond just the Arab world, and you being American will add to the sensationalism, perhaps even become the centerpiece of the story," said Darius, clearly having thought of this before. "The world will take notice. Every newspaper and television channel. Do you see, Jan? We will all be on the main stage of the world. If it succeeds, it will elevate the images of both Ephraim and myself in a world that is increasingly changing the old balances of power between men and women. It will allow Ephraim and I to perhaps resolve this conflict without either of us losing face, to compromise without compromising. It is the only way this will work. Perception is everything. If it succeeds, of course."

"If it succeeds . . ." Jan said to herself when the Sheikh stood and walked a few paces away to take a phone call. She watched him as he spoke quietly in Arabic, and then she smiled at the dark-eyed veiled woman who'd graciously dried her feet and was holding Jan's shoe out like this was a Cinderella story. "Oh, no, you don't need to do that," Jan said, reaching to take the shoe away and put it on herself.

"It is my privilege," said the attendant quietly. She glanced into Jan's eyes. "There is no dishonor or disgrace in serving another."

Jan frowned as she held the eye contact, and the moment stayed with her even as the attendant quickly looked down, slipped the shoes onto Jan's feet, and then backed away toward a black Land Cruiser that had accompanied the Sheikh's Range Rover. These are the people you'd be serving, it suddenly occurred to her. These men and women, their children, and generations to come. It would prevent a war, elevate the confidence and self-image of these people. Could you make it about them and not you?

Easier said than done, she reminded herself. You have an ego too. You are ambitious in your own way. Think of what happens if you go ahead with this. You'd be a sensation, like Darius said. A queen with two kings by her side? Magazine covers? Feature stories? Public opinion from all corners of the globe?

There would be those who'd call her a slut and a whore, but others who'd call her a role model, a shining example of how far women had come in the world.

And even if the idea was a bust—which it probably would be—she'd learn something about the world of shared marriages, wouldn't she? Worst case she'd get a double-divorce and a book deal.

Stop it, she told herself. Before you can even consider yourself capable of being a ruler, you need to handle your own ego. It may start off being about you, but eventually it would have to be about a greater good. And it would be a great good, wouldn't it? You're being given a chance to resolve a brewing conflict that could save thousands of lives! To prevent a war with marriage? Didn't great women over the centuries do just that?

So as insane as it sounds, wouldn't it be more insane not to consider walking down this path? What if I say no and six months later Habeetha and Noramaar go to war? What if Saudi Arabia decides to intervene? What if the U.S. decides to send troops?! What if in some twisted way, saying no would result in American soldiers getting killed yet again in some faraway desert?! Was it now her duty to walk down this path? To at least try?!

But even if I wanted to, could I actually do it? Two men? One of whom just kidnapped me? And I haven't even met the other! Can I agree to consider sleeping with a man I haven't even met yet?! What about marrying a man I haven't even seen!? Who does that?!

Every woman in an arranged marriage has done

exactly that, she reminded herself, thinking back to that old tradition, something that existed in every culture and society to some degree, even in the highest reaches of the so-called "civilized" societies of Europe and America.

Jan looked at her shoes as she thought, the shimmering waters of the Golden Oasis silently watching her. It really felt like she was at a crossroads. She thought about the logical decision, which would be to point those shoes back to reality, back to the United States, to her safe little office in Pittsburgh, her research, lesson-plans, student-faculty barbecues. Then she looked into the waters of the oasis, imagining what her life would be like if she went forward. Immediately she felt it within her again, like she'd already made a decision just by going this far. She was already in this new world. The question now was not if she'd do it, but how she'd do it.

Oh, God, she thought. If these two kings are so proud that they'd risk war and bloodshed rather than back down and lose face in public, then how are they going to manage their possessiveness when it comes to sharing a woman?! Was that what Darius meant when he said she was the battleground?! That these powerful men would have to battle their own emotions even as she fought to balance their pride along with her own goddamn sanity?! Oh, God, what was she getting into?! Two men? Two men! What would her mother think?

To hell with Mom, what do I think?! Isn't this the true test of my beliefs? It's easy to sit in a sterile university office and talk about theories and history, about how our ancestors shared close romantic and sexual relationships with several members of their tribes, how those shared marriages only became taboo over the past few hundred years. Can I walk the talk now? Can I experiment on myself, see if it really is possible, if my body and mind and heart can handle this without guilt, shame, fear even?

Jan looked towards the Sheikh again and realized he'd been off the phone for some time and was looking over at her, as if he was trying to figure out what was going through her mind. She gave him a half-smile, and he returned it, his eyes narrowing slightly, a knowing look passing between them. A look that said there's only so much that can be said in words. The rest needs to be played out in experience.

That's what you meant by 'if it succeeds,' didn't you? she thought as she looked away and closed her eyes tight. You know that if we enter into this game, the emotions will be real—which means they will be unpredictable. You know that if this begins, it's not clear how it will end.

And then immediately Jan knew what came next. The third piece in this puzzle. The third player in this game. That was the next move, as ridiculous as it seemed.

12

"**T**his is ridiculous," Jan said as she looked at the blue gown that had been fitted just right around her waist, hips, and chest but somehow floated beautifully around her shoulders and down to her feet. It was elegant, regal, and somehow sexy. It was a gown made for a queen. Or for a royal slut. "I can't do this. What was I thinking?"

"You do not need to do anything," the Sheikh said quietly from beyond the thick purple curtains that separated the dressing area from the rest of her sprawling chambers in the Eastern Wing of Noramaar's Royal Palace. "We are simply attending a charity gala in London. You are my guest, and donors at my level are allowed many guests. Besides, this is a closed event. No press. Just the Foundation overseers, the top donors, and their guests. Now, may I enter and look at you? The Royal Tailors have spent a week slaving over this gown, and I would like to see why they are so proud of their creation."

"You may enter," she said with a flourish that surprised her. The gown was tight in just the right places, and Jan could feel a confidence she didn't know existed in this body of hers. Yes, she'd felt sexy in dresses before, but this was different. This was more than just feeling sexy. There was an excitement so strong it almost made her sick. Or perhaps it was the thought that she was about to get on the Sheikh's private jet and fly across the world to jolly old England, to a closed-door, black-tie, charity gala, where Sheikh Ephraim would be in attendance. Oh, God, what was she doing?! Especially in this dress?! Was she a royal whore? Nope, she wasn't royalty yet, so if anything, she was just a common slut!

"Ya Allah," Darius shouted when he pushed aside the curtains and rested his eyes upon her curves in that shimmering blue gown. "I will have to chop off the hands of the Royal Tailors so they never make a dress like this for another."

"Um, then they'd never be able to make me a dress like this again, your dumbass highness," Jan said, twirling once and marveling at how the skirts of the gown rose up just enough to show off the long side-slit that was beautifully hidden but breathtakingly revealing when seen. "And I kinda like it. Can I keep it?"

But the Sheikh did not answer, and when Jan looked upon his face she saw the cloud that had descended upon it. She didn't need to ask what was wrong. It was obvious: The man was jealous. Jealous out of his goddamn mind.

He turned from her and stormed to the open balcony, gazing across the back courtyards and towards the banks of the Golden Oasis, which looked dark ocher in the light of the setting sun. She could feel the conflict in him, like a coiled dragon within his body and heart. Somehow it excited her, and she stood still for a moment, wondering if she was evil to the core, a sick, twisted woman for actually being excited from watching the Sheikh get pissed off and jealous.

They'd spent a week together, but they hadn't made love again since the wild encounter on the plane. They'd been close, affectionate, passionate even. But they'd let the tension build and build, as if they both knew it was needed to get them through this first and perhaps toughest hurdle. It was clear by now that they felt the beginnings of something for one another, and without saying it they both knew that if their one-on-one bond became too strong too fast, it might prevent them from proceeding. And what came next was crucial. Could Jan feel a genuine attraction towards Ephraim? Could she follow up on it, even though she already felt the beginnings of a strong connection with Darius? Would Ephraim feel it? And if Ephraim and Jan did both feel it, could Darius get past that? Could she get past it?

So many questions. And they can't be answered with theories and talking, Jan thought as she held herself back from walking to the Sheikh and embracing him like she wanted. They can only be answered in the real world, in the body, in the flesh.

And so she stayed still, in front of the diamond-and-ruby encrusted mirror, and looked at herself standing there all alone, in a dress fit for a queen. She stood there and looked into her own eyes, wondering if she even recognized herself.

"Who are you?" she whispered to herself as that sliver of dark excitement went through her and she saw her own lips curl into a smile that almost frightened her. "Who are you now?"

13

"**I** know who you are," said Ephraim as he shook her gloved hand and bowed his head just a touch. His heavy mane was oiled and coiffed, and his dark green eyes sparkled as he glanced down into her eyes, the sparkling chandeliers of the ballroom almost blinding Jan as she looked up at him. "I have read some of your papers."

Jan felt the blood rush to her face as she blinked and did her best not to pull her hand away from the muscular, dark-eyed Sheikh Ephraim. He was in a dark maroon tuxedo with a thin black tie that made his hard frame look wider and more foreboding. Ephraim was not as tall as Darius, but he was thicker and heavier, all muscle, with features rougher and more rugged than those of the handsome, always composed Darius.

"How many of her papers have you read, Ephraim?" said Darius, who seemed just a bit on edge in a way that both surprised and excited Jan as she watched the two Sheikhs face each other in the ballroom of the Royal Yacht Club in London. "Because she has published thirty-three of them, and if I remember correctly, you didn't finish reading a single book at Oxford."

Ephraim shrugged, not missing a beat, his eyes locked in on Jan's as she felt her heart race. "I was developing other skills at Oxford," he said with a smirk. A quick glance at Darius, then all his focus back on Jan. "No, I have certainly not bothered to read all thirty-three papers. But enough to make me curious."

"Curious about what?" said Jan, blinking and looking past Ephraim to where the band were tuning their violins on the low-set stage at the far end of the ballroom as men in tuxedos and women in gowns began to file onto the dance floor while a buzz rose up around them. Or perhaps the buzz was inside her. Hard to tell. Oh, God.

"About why Darius is so interested in the two of us making our acquaintance," Ephraim said with shocking nonchalance.

Jan turned a bright red, and she hoped her makeup and the flattering yellow light would cover her color. She wanted to glare at Darius, but she held her polite smile and continued to look at Ephraim, who was clearly trying to rattle her. *Already the game has begun*, she thought. *Except I have no clear idea what the game is, let alone how to play it. Perhaps I'm the game. Perhaps I'm the one being played.*

"He wants us to make our acquaintance because I asked him for an introduction, Sheikh Ephraim," Jan said smartly, noting from the corner of her eye how

Darius glanced at her as if he was surprised at her quick reply. "I hoped I might be able to interview you."

"Interview me or study me, Professor?" said Ephraim, that smirk back on his face. "You are not a journalist. Though you are not quite a scientist either, so I suppose I should not take it to mean I am some creature of the desert to be examined as a curiosity."

"Enough talk," said Darius, cutting in and slipping his arm around her waist in a way that made Jan inhale sharply when she saw Ephraim's eyes narrow as he glanced down at her breasts, then at Darius's arm, and finally up into Jan's eyes. "Ms. Johansen and I are about to christen the dancefloor. Come, my lady."

"Um, I don't dance," Jan whispered as she felt Ephraim's eyes still on her as Darius whisked her away towards the center of the dancefloor as the sea of coiffed and perfumed aristocrats and benefactors parted for the two of them. "And why did you pull me away? I thought the entire point of this was to meet Ephraim."

"I will lead you, and we will dance magnificently," Darius said firmly. Then he looked down into her eyes, and she saw that flash of possessiveness. "As for your second point, the answer is yes. The point was to meet Ephraim, and you have met him. Now we dance, we visit with the chairperson of the Foundation, pick at the awful British finger-food, and then ride our chariot back to the hotel."

She frowned as she felt his grip tighten around her waist. The band had started up, the violins pulling them into a comfortable, gliding motion as the Sheikh remained true to his word and led her so well that Jan actually felt like she might have enjoyed dancing in the past if she'd had a partner like Darius.

A polite round of applause and some soft whispers, and then the other distinguished couples joined Jan and the Sheikh on the floor. Soon Jan was surrounded by men and women swinging and smiling as the band switched to a lively tune to loosen up the crowd, and eventually she realized she was actually enjoying herself. She laughed as the Sheikh twirled and spun her, gasped as he dipped and pulled her back into him, clapped and cheered when he took a few steps back and showed off some moves that surprised and delighted the crowd.

From the corner of her eye she thought she saw Ephraim standing by the bar, sipping a drink and watching her with that self-satisfied smirk on his dark face, but she was breathless and excited from the action on the dancefloor and she didn't think much of it. It did occur to her briefly that Darius might be putting on a bit of a show to get to Ephraim, but she pushed away the thought. Why would Ephraim get jealous. He didn't even know her, did he? He didn't know Darius's plan, did he? Did he?

She laughed as Darius dipped her again as the music reached its crescendo and the dance ended. Suddenly all that talk back in Noramaar seemed faraway and ludicrous, like a dream, and she joined the rest of the couples clapping for the band and each other.

Though this feels like a dream too, she thought as the Sheikh led her off the dancefloor and towards the far end of the bar. He pointed at the bartender and snapped his fingers, and the mustachioed man nodded and quickly poured an iced-tea with lemon for the Sheikh and a glass of white wine for Jan.

"No, I think I'll stay away from alcohol for the moment," Jan said, smiling at the bartender and pointing at Darius's drink. "One of those for me too. Easy on the lemon, though."

"You do not need to follow Darius's code of conduct even if you are his guest, Ms. Johansen," came Ephraim's deep, mocking voice from the other end of the bar. He strode over to them and tapped the bar twice with his heavy knuckles as the bartender quickly made him a fresh drink. "And if you are afraid that he will get you drunk and have his way with you, I can assure you that you have nothing to fear from the good Sheikh Darius. His conduct with women is beyond reproach." He glanced at Darius. "At least when Darius himself is sober."

Jan caught the way Darius flinched, and she turned to him and smiled. "Wait, you used to drink?"

"That is an overstatement," said Darius. "I experimented with alcohol once when we were at university." He returned Jan's smile and then locked eyes with Ephraim. "Once."

Ephraim smiled. "A king has to try everything once, right, Darius?" His eyes flicked to Jan and then back to Darius. "Or twice?"

Jan felt Darius's body tighten next to her, but she couldn't quite figure out why. The dynamic between these two Sheikhs puzzled her. She knew they'd been at Oxford together, and being kings of neighboring Islamic kingdoms, would have certainly crossed paths often over the years. But the energy between them was mystifying: It certainly wasn't enmity or hatred. She got the sense that these two men might have been great friends under ordinary circumstances, which got her even more puzzled when she remembered that they had been trading threats of war in public for the past three years.

But right now they aren't in the public view, she realized when she remembered that there were no reporters or journalists or even official photographers at the event. She figured it was because many of the Foundation's benefactors had donated anonymously and wished to remain anonymous, so that was not too unusual. What was unusual was that these two Sheikhs seemed to be playing two games: One in public, with the Middle Eastern media, in view of their people; and one in private, where whatever they'd shared in the past was a factor.

At some point these private and public games will

become one, Jan thought as she looked at Darius stir his tea while Ephraim clinked the ice in his glass. The only question is whether I'm stupid enough to still be around when it happens.

14

Do not be stupid, Ephraim, he told himself as he clinked the ice cubes in his glass and watched Darius and Jan greet the chairperson of the Foundation. Darius was playing his role as the good and elegant Sheikh, while Jan was smiling bright and nodding graciously. What role was she playing? Did she even know this was a game?

But you know it is a game, Ephraim. So do not be stupid. Darius has brought this woman here for one reason: To meet you. It is not clear why he is doing this, but there can be no doubt he is parading her in front of you, his royal arm around her waist, her curves on display in a gown that looks suspiciously like it has been created for her by Noramaar's Royal Tailors. He has already slept with her—that much is clear from the way they danced, they way they look at each other. Yet I see a deep tension in Darius when the three of us are together. I can sense that a part of him wants to take her away from my presence, while another part wants to . . . what, push her toward me? Pull me toward her? What is your game, good Sheikh Ephraim? What are you thinking?

As he watched Jan and Darius, Ephraim's thoughts drifted back to that night at Oxford, when Darius was drunk out of his young mind and Ephraim had grudgingly left the party and helped the stumbling king back to their residence buildings.

"Ya Allah, never again," Darius had slurred as the two young Sheikhs took the solid wooden stairs up to the third floor of the old manor house on the eastern edge of the Oxford campus. "I blame you, Ephraim. You did this."

Ephraim had laughed. "If I recall, it was you who insisted that a king must try everything once, so he might gather experience and wisdom."

Darius had stopped outside the dark oak door to his room and pointed at the ceiling with a flourish. "That is correct. Wisdom comes from experience, and tomorrow I will be wiser! Wonderful! My own wisdom already astounds me, so I cannot wait for tomorrow!"

"What are you two princes laughing about?" came a female voice from down the hallway just then, and Ephraim and Darius had turned to see the tall Norwegian heiress who was a year ahead of them at Oxford. She'd been at the party earlier, but had left to work on her final thesis. She wore red silk pajamas and a flimsy white t-shirt through which her nipples were clearly visible, and her blue eyes sparkled as they alternated between the two Sheikhs. Ephraim had slept with her several times the previous year, and in fact he'd wanted more than just sex. But she'd refused, saying she was committed to marrying a Swedish millionaire so that their two families' business empires could be merged down the line. What was she doing in the hallway near Darius's room, Ephraim had wondered at the time, a cloud of jealousy whipping through him.

"Darius was just saying he needs to try everything at least once," Ephraim had said, frowning as he glanced at her erect nipples pushing against the thin cloth of her t-shirt. "What do you think about that?"

"I think it's a fine idea. So what's on the agenda for tonight's first-time experience?" she'd said, coming closer.

Ephraim's jaw had tightened as he noted the way Darius was looking at her. Had Darius fucked her too? Was she here to see him? Had she chosen Darius over Ephraim? Did she like his cock better? Did she love him?

The thoughts had rushed through Ephraim in a fury, and it had ignited a wild competitiveness in him. Even then he knew it wasn't so much about that Norwegian heiress as much as it was about something else: Competition. The thrill of the fight. The need to win. Ephraim wouldn't have given the woman a second thought if he hadn't sensed that she might prefer Darius to him, that she might be willing to give

Darius more than she'd given him, that Darius had satisfied her more than Ephraim had, that Darius had made her come harder.

One look at Darius and Ephraim sensed it in him as well: That feeling of competition. Darius's jaw was fixed and hard, his green eyes focused as if the adrenaline had sobered him up. Slowly Darius turned his head and made eye contact with Ephraim before glancing back at the smiling heiress in her silk pajamas.

"I think you know what is on the agenda," Darius had growled, stepping forward and grabbing the woman by the hair as she gasped in shock, her mouth hanging open. But Darius stopped short of kissing her. He held her tight, glanced at Ephraim, and then back into the woman's blue eyes, which had widened at first but were now narrowing and showing that sparkle once more. "Yes?"

Ephraim had stared at Darius, then at the woman as the adrenaline shot through his own body. But it was more than just adrenaline, he knew. Something else was fueling his arousal, and Ephraim knew that Darius could feel it too. Was Darius more attracted to her because he knew that Ephraim had slept with her? Was there something about the two of them fighting over something that got both of them going? Fighting over territory? Possessions? Who knew. All Ephraim knew at the time was that if this woman nodded her head and said yes, this was going to happen. A one-time experience.

Ephraim was broken out of the daydream by the sound of applause, and he looked toward the stage to see the good Sheikh Darius stepping up to accept some kind of award for his donation. Ephraim scanned the crowd and quickly found Jan, his cock stiffening when he caught a glimpse of her from behind, the rounds of her bottom perfect and pronounced in that regal blue gown as she clapped her gloved hands along with the crowd.

Yes, he thought as he drained his drink and turned to the bar, his frown deepening. There is no doubt Darius is recalling that experience and wants me to recall it too. But why? Has it something to do with the woman's views on shared marriages? But what sense would that make? The only shared marriages in our world involve one man and multiple women. This does not make sense, unless . . . unless Darius actually believes . . . ya Allah, no. That is too radical. Too much. Sharing a woman for a night is one thing. But sharing her for longer? Sharing her for more than just sex? Sharing her for . . . ever? Forever?

A chill ran through Ephraim as he tapped his knuckles on the oakwood bar and asked for a glass of iced-tea. The thought had crossed his mind when he'd read Jan's research, and now, after seeing Jan, the way she carried herself, the way she'd responded to him calm-

ly after he'd tried to rattle her . . . yes, now Ephraim
was forced to consider the thought again, that this
really might be Darius's plan. After all, Ephraim knew
enough about history to understand how marriages created political alliances, how a strategic marriage could prevent a war. And it didn't take much
to understand what it might mean for two Sheikhs
to marry one woman: They could turn tradition on
its ear, shock and delight the world, make Noramaar
and Habeetha the toast of the world's media! A wild
idea, but not impossible. Was that seriously Darius's
game? Did he seriously believe such a plan could work
out over the long term? And what about Jan? What
did she think? What did she even know?

Yes, what about her? She was the biggest unknown,
was she not? And Ephraim could not consider anything before knowing more about her, before knowing her. All of her. Inside and outside.

So Ephraim took a breath as he glanced at the tall
glass of iced-tea in front of him. Then he reached into
the inner pocket of his maroon jacket and pulled out
a small vial. "The sweet nectar of our shared land," he
muttered as he poured the *aruha* extract into the tea
and stirred it carefully. "All right, Darius. I will play.
But not by your rules. I will not politely step onto the
dancefloor and ask to cut in. I will step in and take
control. On my terms."

He straightened his tie and took the glass over to

where Jan stood, looking deep into her eyes as he watched her drink it. She frowned after taking a sip, licking her lips and cocking her head as she looked at the glass. Then she looked back at him, holding the eye contact even though he thought he saw a streak of fear whip through her behind those big brown eyes. A moment's hesitation, and then she gulped the rest of the glass down and handed it back to him.

"I must be insane," he heard Jan whisper as she leaned against him, and a chill ran through Ephraim when he realized that ya Allah, she knows what is happening and she is going forward anyway! She is not some innocent in the game. She is a player in the game.

She might even be in control.

15

I've lost control, Jan thought. She blinked three times and licked her lips, taking in the now-familiar after-taste of the sweet *aruha*. She'd tasted it in the first sip of the tea Ephraim had offered, and she'd gulped it down anyway. Truthfully, that's why she drank the tea—after all, she didn't particularly like iced tea.

Yes, I've lost control of myself, my mind, my grip on reality, she thought again as she tried to get her bearings. Was she on a plane? Already in Habeetha? Somewhere else?

I'm in a bed, she realized as her senses came back to her and she felt the pillows beneath her head and the cool sheets against her body. Against her naked body.

"Oh God, no!" she cried out when she realized she didn't have a shred of clothing on beneath the sheets. "Oh, please no!"

Jan sat up straight and pulled the sheets up over her bare breasts as panic gave way to a sinking feeling of dread. Had this really happened? She didn't remember a thing, but she was in what looked like a hotel room, naked to the toes after being drugged by a Sheikh who was king of Sin City, Arabia!

He raped me, she thought in anger as she carefully touched herself between her legs to see if she was sore, if she was bleeding, if that sick animal's semen was oozing out of her after he'd taken what he wanted when she was powerless to resist. She didn't have any soreness or pain, and there was no blood or semen on her or in her that she could feel. After making sure the bedroom was empty, she pulled the sheets away and examined herself and then the bedsheets beneath her bottom. No bruises on her smooth, creamy skin. No damp spots or stains on the pristine white sheets.

"That doesn't prove anything," she muttered, fighting back a dreadful sense of guilt as a part of her whispered that she'd slurped down that *aruha* drug like a goddamn witch-whore and put herself in a position of absolute vulnerability. What did she expect was going to happen? Another round of hot sex on a private plane? Nope. You get used like a harlot while you're passed out. It's his fault for doing it, but you're still a goddamn fool.

Jan looked around the room again. Certainly a hotel room. There was a window at the far end, but the curtains were drawn. She looked for a phone. No phone. Cameras on the walls? No cameras. What about clothes? Um, no clothes anywhere in sight. Neither hers nor his. Where the hell was she?

She swung her legs off the bed and wrapped the sheets around her, carefully standing and bumbling over to the window. She took a breath and pulled the curtains away, squinting and turning her head when the sun hit her full. When she got her sight back she looked out, letting forth a deep sigh when she saw the Tower of London in the distance. She was still in England.

"What do you think he will do?" came the voice from behind her, and Jan was so startled she almost dropped the sheets.

She turned on her feet, making sure not to fall flat on her face as she trampled on the sheets and tried to look calm and composed in the presence of the man who'd just raped her. "How could you?" she said, frowning when she saw that Ephraim was still wearing that maroon tuxedo, tie included. "Have you no shame? What kind of a man does that?"

Ephraim didn't flinch. "What kind of a man did you think I was when you drank the *aruha*? When you knowingly drank the *aruha*, I should add."

Jan blinked hard and swallowed. "I don't know what you mean. All I know is that you drugged me last night, and now I'm naked in a hotel room with no memory of what happened."

Jan blinked again as she looked at Ephraim. He seemed calm, in control, his dark green eyes unwavering and alert. She glanced at his clothes again. The shirt had lost some of its crispness and the jacket had a definite crease in it, like he'd been wearing those clothes all night. But that still didn't prove anything. He'd done it. Hadn't he?

Is he trying to mess with my head, she wondered as she forced herself to look into his eyes, guilt creeping through her when she realized she didn't feel the hate and anger she wanted to feel. Was it the drug that was numbing her? Or was it the look in his eyes—a look that whispered the truth: that perhaps he wasn't an unhinged rapist, that perhaps he had simply decided to enter the game on his own terms.

Ephraim smiled, his thick red lips parting, his perfect teeth shining white against the dark stubble that lined his strong jaw. He shook his head while holding the eye contact, his long black hair looking like a stallion's mane, his eyes narrowing as he laughed. "Those are indeed the facts, I suppose. You were drugged, and now you are naked in a hotel room. As for your memory . . . yes, the strain of *aruha* that grows in Habeetha is more potent, and it does cause a blackout effect. Too bad. I am sure you would enjoy the memories of last night, Professor Janice." He paused. "May I call you Jan?"

She snorted. "You may not call me anything. We don't know each other, and we never will, after what you've done."

"I disagree," Ephraim said drolly, raising an eyebrow and rubbing his stubble. "We already know a lot about each other simply from our actions."

"What actions? I didn't—"

"You knew what was in that tea, and you drank it anyway. That means you'd tasted *aruha* before, and since it only grows in the desert around the Golden Oasis, it must have been Darius who gave it to you the first time." Ephraim paused, that smirk returning as his eyes gleamed. "The good Sheikh Darius. Did he tell you I was the evil king in this story? Are you sure you know who is the good king and who is the evil one?"

Jan took a breath and frowned as her head spun. A part of her still couldn't fathom why she'd downed that tea when she tasted the drug in it. Did she want to be powerless and vulnerable? Did she want to give up control and let the so-called evil Sheikh have his way with her? Was it because of the madness of what she was getting herself into, the strange mix of guilt and excitement that was impelling her forward even though by all logic she was in a situation that was disgusting at best and deadly at worst? After all, these were kings threatening to send their armies into battle for the future of their kingdoms! Would they even think twice about manipulating and using her, disposing of her if it suited them?

"He told me . . ." she started to say. "He told me . . ."

"Say no more," Ephraim whispered, still smirking though his eyes revealed something that made Jan shiver—and not in fright but excitement. "Your actions have told me enough. The game is on and you are playing it, Professor Johansen. We are all playing it. Darius set this in motion, but all three of us have made conscious, deliberate moves. I made the move of drugging you. You made the move of allowing yourself to be drugged. Now it is time for Darius's next move. I am hitting the ball back to him."

Jan frowned, pulling the sheets tight around her curves and then glaring up at him as that sense of excitement grew to the point where all fear was gone and it was just excitement. "I'm the ball in this game? Did you just call me a ball?"

Ephraim took a step forward, his dark eyes shining as he cocked his head. Slowly he walked toward her, and now Jan could smell him, an earthy, heavy musk of sandalwood and desert oak that overwhelmed her senses as she felt her nipples stiffen beneath the sheets. What was she doing? Was she actually flirting with this asshole?

Slowly the dark Sheikh circled her as she stood there barefoot and vulnerable, and the arousal began to build as her thighs tingled, her buttocks tightened, her toes curled. When he got so close she could feel his clean, warm breath on her bare neck, the wetness began to flow from her secret space, and when he brought his lips close to her face, she opened her mouth and gently sighed as she felt herself close to losing control.

"There will come a time when I shall call you what I want, when I want," he whispered without touching her. He glanced into her eyes and she almost swooned as she sensed the movement in his fitted maroon pants as he stiffened, as if his cock was straining to be unleashed, as if her oozing cunt was calling out from beneath those white sheets. "But for now, I will call you Helen." He took a long breath and smiled tightly, as if it was taking all his willpower to not touch her, to not take her. "My attendants will bring your clothes back shortly. There will be a car waiting for you whenever you choose to leave. Good day . . . Helen. It is time for you to return to the good Sheikh Darius."

Jan blinked and frowned as the Sheikh suddenly stepped away from her and walked across the room toward the door. She blinked again when she saw the way his trousers were peaked at the front. Clearly he was aroused beyond belief. The way he'd backed off confused her even more than him calling her Helen when he knew her real name was Jan. Helen? Who was Helen?

And then it hit her. Helen of Troy. The woman who'd been kidnapped by a king, starting a war that changed the course of history. Suddenly she knew he hadn't raped her. He hadn't even touched her. And something about the way he'd backed off despite his arousal told her that perhaps he hadn't even undressed her himself, had perhaps not even taken the liberty of looking at her naked body when she was passed out.

Helen of Troy. That was his first move, wasn't it?

Ephraim wanted to see if he could provoke Darius into doing something rash, perhaps even violent. That's why he wanted her to think she'd been raped. Yes, of course! She'd go running back to the good Sheikh Darius, tell him what the evil King Ephraim had done, and spark a war! Was Ephraim testing Darius to see if Jan meant anything to him? Was he testing Jan to see what she'd do? Was he testing himself? All three at once? Who knew?

Only one way to find out, she decided as the blood rushed to her head. Only one way.

"Helen of Troy wasn't sent back, you know," she called after him, her heart almost beating its way out of her chest when she realized what she was doing.

The Sheikh stopped at the door, his broad back to her, his thick long hair looking wild against the dark red of his jacket. Slowly he turned, and it took all of Jan's strength to stay focused on his face and not the enormous peak at the front of his trousers. "Ya Allah," he whispered as his jaw went tight and his eyes blazed a deep green. Slowly he looked her up and down, his lips trembling as he clenched his fists. "Careful," he whispered. "Once you step all the way into the arena, there is no stepping out until the game is finished."

He took a step and stopped, his eyes giving her one last chance to take back the move she was making. But Jan was outside herself now, logic and common sense thrown to the wind, her entire being operating on nothing but instinct and intuition. And though every part of her brain screamed for her to stop, her body wouldn't listen, and slowly her fingers loosened their grip on those sheets.

The soft white cloth slipped off her shoulders, past her breasts, finally falling away, leaving her naked as the day she was born, smooth white breasts with peaked red nipples, her dark brown triangle shamelessly exposed to the man who'd abducted her. She could smell herself, wet and ready, hot and heavy, and as the Sheikh's entire body tensed up visibly, she whispered from a part of her that she didn't know existed:

"I think I'm already in the arena, Sheikh Ephraim. I'm already in it."

16

He came to her slowly, deliberately, stripping as he approached. First the dark red jacket dropped to the carpet, then the fitted white shirt was unbuttoned and removed. He stopped in front of her, bare-chested and hard, unbuckling his belt as Jan watched in a state somewhere between paralyzing shock and overwhelming arousal.

Oh, God, what am I doing, came the desperate thought when she felt her own wetness dripping down the insides of her quivering thighs as she stared at Ephraim's thick brown pectorals, heavy and glistening in the yellow light, his tight dark nipples like black moons, his abdomen built with ridges of dark muscle, a sharp treasure trail of coarse hair running from his belly button down the front of his pants.

Jan swooned when Ephraim slid his heavy leather belt through the loops and dropped his pants, smoothly stepping out of them and straightening to full height, baring his broad shoulders, cracking his neck as if stretching before a fight. He stood before her in just his black underwear, which was straining to hold the heavy swell of his crotch. Jan could clearly see the outline of his cock, coiled like a python, thick like a log, its head pushing against the black silk of his underwear like it was trying to burst free and take her. His thighs were like tree-trunks, rippled with muscle, lined with veins, and Jan swallowed hard as she tried to push away a vivid image of Ephraim's beast of a cock disappearing between her legs as those powerful thighs of his pumped her so hard she screamed. What was happening to her? What kind of a woman had she become? Or was she always this woman?

You're allowing yourself to wake up, that's all, she told herself as she trembled from the sight of Ephraim slowly pushing the waistband of his underwear down. This is what you've studied and researched, haven't you? That for millions of years women were taken by multiple men of the tribe, that it was a survival mechanism, selected by evolution. You know that what you're feeling lives inside every woman, but today's morals force us all to deny those instincts, to suppress those needs, to reject even the suggestion that we can be strong, ambitious, intellectual women in the workplace but still get aroused by those old instincts which allowed us to survive and thrive in ancient societies.

"Oh, shit," she muttered when Ephraim's cock finally sprang into view as he pushed his tight black underwear down past those muscular thighs and tossed them away. "Oh, God, Ephraim."

"You know I did not touch you last night," the Sheikh whispered, his voice thick with arousal as he stroked his cock until it curved upwards, supremely hard, its dark red tip swollen and oozing, his heavy balls looking full and loaded as his erection brought them into view. "But I am going to touch you now. Touch you all over. Outside, and inside. Deep inside. All the way inside."

Jan felt herself nodding as she watched his cock gently bounce as he approached. She could smell her own sex mixing with his earthy musk, and when he got so close she could feel the tip of his cock brush against the delicate hairs of her feminine, her throat almost closed up with need.

Ephraim looked into her eyes as he reached down and grasped his cock firmly around the shaft. Then he slowly rubbed the head of his beast against her pubic curls, finding her clit and pressing against it with his cock in a way that made her moan as the heat roared through her like a desert storm. They still hadn't even kissed, and the only contact was the tip of his cock against her throbbing clit, and it was so delicate, so perfect, so incredibly poignant, that without understanding what was happening, Jan shuddered and shivered and suddenly, out of nowhere, realized she was about to have a massive orgasm.

She opened her mouth to speak as her eyes went wide in shock. But the words didn't come, and instead it was Ephraim who spoke.

"Come for me," he whispered as he rotated his cock-head against her pulsing nub, flicking her stiff little bean with his thick head. "Look into my eyes and come for me, Jan. I said look at me. Look at me as you come."

She could barely hear him as her orgasm roared through her body, but somehow she managed to focus on his eyes, those dark green embers bearing down on her as her climax whipped her into a paralyzed frenzy. She was coming hard, after barely being touched, before even being kissed. Coming hard. Coming for him. For the Sheikh, for Ephraim, at his command.

Which one is he, came the thought as she finally collapsed against him as her climax brought her to her knees. The evil Sheikh or the good king? Which one is he?

17

"**W**here is she?" Sheikh Darius asked the frightened attendant who was kneeling before him in the heavily-carpeted presidential suite of the London Grand Plaza hotel. "Where has Ephraim taken her?"

"La 'aerif," said the attendant, one of Ephraim's men, who'd been dragged to Darius's suite by the Sheikh's bodyguards in the middle of the night. He was the only member of Ephraim's entourage that Darius's men had managed to seize. The rest seemed to have vanished just like Ephraim and Jan. "I do not know, Sheikh Darius! I am only a baggage-handler for Sheikh Ephraim! I do not even enter his presence! I know nothing! I only know that all the Sheikh's entourage are gone, and I was ordered to stay behind to make sure the luggage was accounted for! I know nothing else, I swear it!"

"Kadhaab," said Darius, glancing at one of his bodyguards and then at the attendant. "Cut off three fingers and then I will ask him again."

"No!" screamed the attendant. "I swear to Allah that I speak the truth!"

"Then Allah will grow your fingers back for you," said Darius. He snapped his fingers at his bodyguard. "Do it."

The bodyguard grabbed the attendant's right arm and pulled out a curved dagger from beneath his jacket as the man began to howl like a caged beast. The bodyguard pushed the attendant face-down on the carpet, pressing the point of his knee into the screaming man's back, pinning him on the floor. The bodyguard positioned the glistening edge of the dagger just beneath the middle knuckles of the man's fingers, and took a long breath before glancing up at the Sheikh.

Darius looked down at the attendant, who was bawling like a child at the Sheikh's feet. Then he grunted softly and gestured to his bodyguard, who exhaled hard and pulled the dagger away before removing his knee from the attendant's back.

"When did Ephraim's private jet take off from Heathrow?" said Darius to another bodyguard as he watched the relieved attendant get ushered to the door and sent on his way. "And can we confirm that Ephraim was actually on board?"

He listened as his men answered the question he'd asked three times over the past hour. Ephraim's jet had taken off shortly after Darius realized Jan was missing. He'd seen the glass of iced-tea with her lipstick on it, and he could smell the *aruha* even before he brought his nose to it. Darius had almost smashed the glass against the table in front of everyone at the gala, but somehow managed to restrain himself long enough to leave the room and make it back to his hotel suite, where he punched the stainless-steel refrigerator so hard the dent showed the outline of each knuckle.

He'd thought of calling the police, but something had stopped him. There was no doubt in his mind that Ephraim had taken Jan, and he suspected that Ephraim had stayed in London while sending his empty jet back to Habeetha in an attempt to make Darius think he'd left. What was he thinking, the arrogant fool?! Was Ephraim hoping that Darius would fly back to Noramaar in a blind rage, order his men to head to Habeetha's Royal Palace, perhaps even order a full-on attack on Habeetha? Perhaps, but unlikely. Ephraim could not seriously expect that Darius would order a military operation over a woman he'd known for a week. No, Ephraim had done it merely as a signal that he was ready to play the game, but on his own terms, that there were no rules, that Darius might have started the game but wasn't going to be able to control every move.

But was this just Ephraim's move, or was it Jan's move as well, the thought had come as Darius went over the events of the night. And then it came to him, and Darius had almost lost his mind when he realized what he'd missed. That glass of iced-tea had been drained to the last drop, and judging by the lingering smell of the *aruha*, there was no way the taste had been disguised well enough for Jan not to notice. Which meant she'd known what was in that glass and she'd gone forward anyway.

It was just after this realization that his bodyguards had dragged in Ephraim's attendant, and Darius was in such a state that he'd been serious about cutting off the poor man's fingers. It was only that last look from his bodyguard that brought the Sheikh back to reality—the reality that he was shaken and turned around, that Ephraim had gotten to him.

And the only reason Ephraim had gotten to him was because Jan had gotten to him. She'd gotten to Darius, and she'd shown that she was ready to step into the arena and play this game with them.

Perhaps she has already stepped into the arena, came the last thought as Darius waved away his men and realized he could do nothing right now but wait. Ya Allah, Professor Johansen. You have stepped in with us, have you not? So I hope you know that now there is no turning back . . .

Not for any of us.

18

She turned her back to Ephraim and curled into a fe-tal position when he placed her on the bed after she came for him and collapsed into his arms. He pulled the covers over her naked body and then lay down beside her, breathing hard as his cock throbbed and his balls clenched tight. Already Ephraim could feel himself fall under her spell—a spell that she perhaps did not even know she was casting upon him, perhaps upon them both! He watched her back rise and fall as she took deep breaths, marveled at the way the silk sheets highlighted her womanly curves, shuddered at the scent of her perfume mixing with the aroma of her wet sex. He was hard and ready, and there was nothing to stop him from pulling those covers off her and taking her hard and fast, any way he want-ed. He'd done it a thousand times, with a thousand different women. But he held back and waited, his chest heaving as he controlled his arousal and lay there beside her.

Ephraim listened to her breathe, and slowly he matched her breath for breath until he could sense their bodies falling into a subtle rhythm even though they lay side by side with no contact and she still had her back to him.

Ya Allah, I feel an attraction, a pull, a magnetic draw to her, Ephraim thought as he marveled at how this woman was somehow controlling him even though in a way she'd lost control of herself. Her orgasm had been real, intense, wild, and it had almost driven Ephraim himself over the edge. But somehow he'd held himself in check and carried her to the bed, laying her down gently instead of pushing her face into the pillow and pumping into her from behind until he exploded into her depths like he wanted.

Now he felt movement as their breathing stayed in rhythm, and he turned his head to see Jan's big brown eyes looking at him. She'd turned on her side to face him, and she looked beautiful in the yellow light of the sun that streamed in from behind. The angle of the sun's rays cast her in a strange golden light, and Ephraim frowned as he was reminded of the shining waters of the Golden Oasis. A chill ran through him when he thought back to what he'd read about Jan, about her research into shared marriages, her belief that humans had evolved as a species who enjoyed multiple sexual partners and formed strong bonds that were more than just one-on-one.

We are all just part of her research, just like she herself is part of her research, he thought. And there is no way to research something like this without immersing yourself into it, without letting yourself go, without giving up control. She knows it. That is why she willingly drank the *aruha*. And that is why Darius has chosen her. The thought had occurred to him several times before, but it did not really hit home until he looked into her brown eyes, took in the sight of her brown curls lit by the morning sun, the sheets draped over her curves in a way that made him think she might be a goddess in human form, sent down to either save them or destroy them.

"Hi," she said softly, blinking once and looking down at the bed before holding the eye contact again. She looked shy, almost ashamed. Was it an act? Did she even know if it was an act?

"Hello," he whispered. "Are you all right?"

She nodded and murmured. Then she shook her head. "I don't know what I am. I don't know who I am. I don't know what I'm doing here."

Ephraim took a breath, frowning as he wondered how to play this. Everything about this woman seemed genuine right then—the orgasm, the confusion, the shame, the uncertainty. But at the same time she'd willingly stepped into this situation, hadn't she? She'd come to London on Darius's arm, allowed Ephraim to take her, and then collapsed into his arms as she came at his command. Who was playing whom? Who was the seducer and who was being seduced?

Who was the researcher and who was the goddamn lab rat? He thought he knew the answer—that all three of them were her lab rats—but he needed to hear her say it. He needed to hear her tell him the truth.

"You are here because you want to be here," he said. "Yes?"

She took a breath and blinked, and there was that flash of shame. But when she looked into his eyes again the shame was gone, as if by an act of her own will. "Yes," she said.

"Why?" Ephraim said firmly.

"Because . . . because . . . oh, God, I don't even know how to explain it. I can't even begin to understand it myself. It seems mad."

"That is a good start to understanding it. Yes, it is mad. Go on. Tell me. Tell me everything. Do not worry about whether it makes sense. Just talk. It is just the two of us." He reached out and touched her brown hair that seemed infused with the gold of sunlight. That chill went through him again as he did it, and he felt her shudder under his careful caress. Would she be honest about why she was here, about what Darius was thinking? Did he even care as he lay here beside her, her scent overwhelming him, just a thin sheet separating her body from his.

"Just the two of us . . ." she whispered, a smile breaking on her pretty round face. "That's what makes it so mad. It's not just the two of us!"

Ephraim exhaled slowly as that chill spread to his entire body, somehow warming him to the core. Now he knew Darius had slept with her. He'd suspected it, but to hear her say it was something else. A flash of anger passed through him, and he hated himself for it. Jealousy? Over a woman you have not even slept with yet? Or is it that fire of competition? "No, it is not just the two of us. And it will never be just the two of us. That is what Darius wants, yes? That is how he convinced you to play this game, yes? He offered you the chance of a lifetime to experiment on yourself, to test your own research, to live your own research." Ephraim paused for a moment as he looked at her expression, which changed for a flash. He needed the full story, even though he suspected he knew. "Something else," he whispered. "He offered you something else? Wealth? Fame?" She stayed quiet and Ephraim blinked and then his eyes stayed steady. "Marriage? He offered you a chance to be the wife of a Sheikh?"

Her eyes narrowed and her smile tightened. She was quiet for a moment, as if wondering how much to tell him. Then she spoke, and from her tone Ephraim knew she'd decided to tell him everything. "The chance to be the wife of two Sheikhs. The chance to prevent a war. The chance to . . . to be queen."

The last word came out in a whisper, and Ephraim saw it on her face as the adrenaline surged through his body. He saw everything in her eyes in that moment. He saw her.

Ambition. Strength. Power. But also compassion and a sense of adventure. He could see now why she said she couldn't understand all the reasons she was doing this: It was because there were many reasons, all of them intertwined, all of them arising from who she was.

"The wife of two Sheikhs, and the queen of two kingdoms," he said, frowning and narrowing his eyes as he caressed her face and then held on to a fistful of her hair as she winced. "So that is why you came here? To seduce me into giving up my kingdom? A little ambitious, don't you think? Not to mention ridiculous."

"Can't blame a girl for trying," Jan whispered through a hesitant smile. "But don't act like you didn't guess this was Darius's idea."

"I guessed no such thing. I assumed Darius sent you to seduce me and then assassinate me with poison or a dagger to my throat."

"Now that's ridiculous," she whispered, looking down at his naked body and then slowly reaching for his cock. "Why would I kill the man who's going to make me his queen?"

"Ya Allah," Ephraim groaned as she stroked his cock with her fingertips, the sensation almost making him come all over the sheets. "Who are you, woman? And why have I not had you tossed out into the street yet?"

"For the same reason you brought me here," Jan

said. "You guessed what Darius is offering. And you're considering taking him up on that offer." Slowly she curled her fingers around his swollen mast, and he groaned and stretched his neck as he went so stiff he almost passed out. "You're considering it very seriously, aren't you? Aren't you?"

She was jerking him back and forth as she spoke, and Ephraim's mind began to spin as a devilish grin broke on his face. He was in it now, he realized. In the goddamn arena. In her goddamn arena!

"Remind me again. What is Darius offering?" he muttered.

"Me," she whispered, leaning up on her elbow as the sheets fell away once more and the golden light bathed her naked body in a glow that Ephraim swore was not of the earth. "He is offering me."

19

Jan wasn't sure if she felt more like a goddess or a whore when she went up on an elbow and pulled the sheets away from her body. She was wet again—that much she couldn't deny. What she was doing aroused her to the point of madness. It must be madness. It had to be madness.

Ephraim felt huge in her hands, his cock so thick she couldn't get her fist to close all the way around. The thought of taking him inside her almost scared her, and she wondered if she'd even be able to stretch that wide. Ephraim wasn't as long as Darius, and shit, Darius had gone into her so damned deep she could still feel him in there. But Ephraim's girth was shocking, and he seemed to be getting bigger and harder as she jerked his dark foreskin to and fro, massaging his mammoth balls as he groaned and grunted.

"Me," she heard herself say. "Darius is offering me."

Ephraim stared at her for a moment, his look hard to interpret. Then he grabbed a fistful of her hair and kissed her hard as he pressed his body against hers, driving his tongue deep into her mouth as he rolled his naked body on top of her, ripping the sheets away from between them as he did it. She gasped as she struggled for breath under his weight, and the sensation of breathlessness combined with the feeling of his cock pressed up against the front of her mound made her moan out loud as she returned his kiss. He began to move on top of her, kissing her with fury, his cock rubbing against her matted pubic hair ferociously, opening up her slit lengthwise, grinding against her clit so hard she almost cried out.

Jan closed her eyes and spread her legs, letting Ephraim kiss her deep and hard as the thought of that heavy cock pushing past her dark nether lips invaded her mind. She moaned as she felt him reach down between them and guide his cockhead to her entrance, and she grimaced as she felt it press against her slick opening.

"I'm going to take you," he whispered into her ear, his voice deep and throaty, his hips poised above her spread-out thighs, his cock pressing its way forward as the folds of her pussy began to open like a flower in the morning as he forced his way in. "But I cannot guarantee I will give you back."

Slowly he pushed into her, her mouth opening in time with the lips of her vagina, her eyes going wide and rolling up in her head at the sensation of being stretched like this was the first time, the first time she'd ever been fucked. He went slow but firm, his powerful hips pushing forward while rotating gently to open the walls of her secret cave.

"So warm," he groaned. "So perfect."

"Oh, God," she muttered through clenched teeth. "Oh, please go slow. I'm so stretched . . . oh, God!"

She came just as the upward curve of Ephraim's cock grazed her secret spot on the front wall of her vagina as it continued its journey into her depths, and the orgasm was so sudden and unexpected that she burst into tears from the sheer confusion.

"Oh, God, what's happening?" she wailed as Ephraim drove his shaft all the way deep and then stopped and held still, looking down into her eyes and caressing her hair as she came again for him.

"Look at me as you come," he growled as he held her hair away from her face and stayed there on top of her, inside her, all around her. "Look at me, Jan."

"What's happening to me?" she gurgled as she stared into his dark green eyes, her orgasm binding her to him in a way she could feel in her depths. "What the hell is happening?"

But Jan knew what was happening, even through that climax. She was opening up in ways more than just physical. Saying the words "Darius has offered me to you" made it real in a way that broke through the chains holding her to the real world, to its morals and beliefs. She was no longer Professor Janice Johansen, and this was no longer the world in which she had a cute little office in Pittsburgh and a classroom full of earnest students with iPhones. She'd stepped into a new world, an old world, a different world. And this world was taking her and would never give her back.

She dug her fingers into Ephraim's thick black hair as the tears rolled down her smooth cheeks, and he smiled down at her as he kissed those tears gently. She could feel his cock flex inside her, but the Sheikh held still, as if he wanted to make sure she was all right. As her orgasm finally released her from its clutches, Jan realized again how deeply she was locked in on Ephraim's eyes, just like she'd been during that first orgasm. She'd read the research about how even strangers who hold steady eye contact for a few minutes develop feelings for each other. Had anyone studied what happened when the strangers were naked and climaxing during that eye contact? The connection scared her, the attraction terrified her, the need overwhelmed her. Was he playing her? Trying to get her to bond with him so he could control her? But the eye-contact trick worked both ways, she remembered as her climax whipped back and forth like the tail of a trapped beast. The bond works both ways.

"I will take you, but I may not be able to give you back," he whispered again as he began to drive those muscular hips, pulling back halfway and then plunging his shaft back into her.

Jan's vagina was opened all the way, stretched wider than she thought possible, and she was wet to the point where Ephraim's girth was sliding in and out effortlessly, even though she could feel him pressing against every part of her inside walls. She spread her legs as far as she could, feeling the last of her inhibitions disappear as she closed her eyes and opened her mouth for his kisses, arched her back so he could suck her hard, pink nipples that were pebbled and erect like large arrowheads, bucked her hips in time with the Sheikh's devastating thrusts.

They moved together in heavy silence, just the sound of their bodies filling the room, his grunts and her whimpers, his growls and her wails, him thrusting and her taking, him driving and her clenching, the Sheikh and the professor, the king and the queen, the players in the game, playing each other, playing themselves.

Jan came again, and this time she didn't need him to tell her to look at him. She did it because she wanted to, did it because she needed to, did it because he'd asked her once and would never need to ask again. She held the eye contact as her climax paralyzed her insides, and in his eyes she saw herself, she thought.

This time the Sheikh fucked her through her orgasm, all way up to heaven and back down to this strange new version of earth she'd slipped into. Then he cried to his god and seized up, his thick neck straining and his strong jaw clenching as his cock drove deep and flexed in preparation.

"Look at me," she whispered as she dug her fingers into his thick hair and clenched her vagina as hard as she could. "Look at me as you come."

The Sheikh roared in pleasure as he rammed into her one last time, and as she felt Ephraim's heavy balls slap against her bare skin and tighten up as he blasted his royal load into her, she grinned up at the ceiling like a madwoman and thought, "Perhaps I don't want you to give me back, Ephraim. Perhaps I don't want you to give me back."

20

What if she does not want to come back to me, Darius wondered as he stared at the silver cup of tea that had once been steaming hot but was now cold and congealed. *Perhaps I should have slept with her again instead of holding myself back. Perhaps I should not have told her everything. Perhaps I should have kept her for myself. Ya Allah, what have I done?*

The Sheikh walked through the long hallway of the southern wing of Noramaar's Royal Palace. A warm breeze oozed its way along the sandstone floor as Darius walked barefoot past these seldom-used rooms of his sprawling palace. This had been where the old Sheikhs of Noramaar had kept the women of their harems, and Darius smiled tightly as he walked into an enclosed courtyard and stopped near the black marble fountain that had been turned off and drained years ago.

There were doors lining the walls that faced the courtyard and fountain, each door painted a different color, some of them with Arabic inscriptions above them, others with symbols, a few with jewels embedded into the old teakwood frames. Darius smiled as he walked to one of the doors and ran his fingers along the inscription. It marked the rooms of the nikaabi, women of the harem who could be shared with guests of the Sheikh so long as the guests were of royal blood. To the left were the rooms of the wakaabi, women who could be offered as rewards for great service to the kingdom. Generals and soldiers were often the ones graced with the gift of a night with the wakaabi.

Finally Darius stopped near the last door, marked with a single diamond. These were the chambers of the shikaabi, the women who came here untouched and would never be touched by any except the supreme Sheikh himself. The king's private stock. Ah, the days of old!

Darius laughed out loud and shook his head as he slammed his palms against the door. The history of man and woman is a strange story, is it not, he thought as he touched his head to the old teakwood and then turned and walked back to the fountain. Adam and Eve. Samson and Delilah. Romeo and Juliet. He laughed again as he thought of those famous couples of myth. The choice to be together brought about the downfall of each of those couples. Had there ever been a great love story that did not end in tragedy?

"Perhaps Jan's theories are correct," he muttered as he looked down over the wall of the black fountain. He saw the levers to turn the water back on, and reached down and slowly released them, smiling as the old pipes gurgled and spat and slowly began to serve up their flow once more. "Perhaps those stories were tragedies because they denied the true history of man and woman, that the story of one man for one woman is a myth, a fiction itself." The Sheikh dipped his hand into the warm waters of the fountain and took a breath. "Of course it is a myth. Look at these rooms of the old harem. Look at the history of infidelity in every culture, society, and household. Look at every ruler from Genghis Khan to Henry the Eighth to Cleopatra to the queens of the Russian empire. They all loved many in their lifetimes, many at the same time. Jan is right. Our true nature is not what we think it is. It is not what we want it to be. She is right. By Allah, she is right!"

And so what will be the story of Jan and Darius and Ephraim, the Sheikh wondered as he stepped into the fountain and stood there, knee deep in the warm water, surrounded by the empty rooms of this palace of fantasy. A tragedy? A farce? Or a love story?

Who knows, he decided as he stepped out and headed back down the sandstone hallways, pulling out his phone along the way and breathing hard as excitement whipped through him. It had been two days since he'd been back in Noramaar, and by now he had no doubt that although Ephraim had taken Jan, she'd also allowed herself to be taken, which meant only one thing: It was time to bring them all together.

But where, he wondered as he dialed Ephraim's private line and waited, wondering why he would expect Ephraim to answer, wondering if he even wanted Ephraim to answer. Where to meet for the first time? A hotel suite? A palace? Europe? South America? Paris? Rio?

The answer came to Darius just as Ephraim answered.

"Two days, Darius?" came Ephraim's deep voice over the phone. "It takes you two days to call to check on your woman?"

"My woman?" said Darius after a moment's pause. "Or our woman?"

Ephraim was silent, but Darius could hear him breathe. "Darius, how well do you know Jan?"

"Well enough. How well do you know her, Ephraim?"

Ephraim laughed, but it was a measured laugh. "Well enough to know that there is much I do not know about her. Do not underestimate her, Darius." He paused and took a breath, his voice going cold in a way that told Darius everything he needed to know about how well Ephraim "knew" Jan by now. "And do not underestimate me, Darius."

"I am wary of making any estimates in this game," whispered Darius. "None of us knows how this will play out."

"Yet each of us knows how we want it to play out, yes?"

Darius frowned as a chill ran through him, the sensation transforming into a steady buzz that troubled him. What was Ephraim saying? That he wanted Jan for himself? Had she told him everything? Had they already fallen in love? The thoughts came quick and hard, and Darius had to take several breaths before he remembered that much of this game would be played in their own heads, with their own emotions, their own doubts and uncertainties, needs and wants, ambitions and aggressions.

"Do we, Ephraim? Do we truly know how we want it to play out?"

Ephraim laughed. "I know how you want it to play out. The three of us, Jan between us." He snorted. "Or Jan on top, rather. Queen of two kingdoms. The grand Sheikha who unites two kingdoms on the brink of war. Ya Allah, I do not know whether to laugh or cry at your childish idealism." A pause and then his pitch deepened. "Perhaps it is indeed time for Noramaar to have a new ruler. Perhaps the good Sheikh Darius has lost his mind. That is what happens when you do away with your harem and spend your days holding your royal cock in your hand and holding these delusions in your mind."

Darius breathed deep and ignored the insult. "And is your harem bringing light and joy to your nights,

Ephraim? If so, please return Jan to me and that will be the end of it."

"Return her to you? She belongs to you?" Ephraim laughed. "Ah, you have showed your hand, Darius. You already feel the possessiveness of a jealous lover. You are not prepared to play this game, because you have allowed her to get under your skin."

Darius smiled, his eyes narrowed and focused. "And you have showed your hand too, Ephraim. I hear it in your voice. She has gotten under your skin too." He paused, and when he heard the heavy silence on the other end of the line, he knew he was right. "Do you see why I chose her? Why it had to be her? Why it had to be a woman who could stand up to the two of us? Stand between us? Stand above us if it comes to that? Do you see, Ephraim?"

Ephraim was silent for a long time, his breathing the only sign that he was still on the line. "Yes," he said finally. "She could stand up to the two of us. Stand between us. Mentally, intellectually, and physically. She could handle us both." He took a trembling breath and whispered softly: "She could take us both."

Darius felt that old excitement of competition roar through him as he gripped his phone so tight it almost cracked down the middle. It was time. Time to take this to the next step and see how it would play out.

"Noor Island," said Darius quietly. "Two days."

Ephraim paused. "Noor Island," he said slowly. "In

the middle of the Golden Oasis? It is too small to land a plane. We can only get there by boat."

"I think you can find a boat, yes?" Darius said. But he knew what Ephraim meant: Noor Island was a patch of raised desert, dead in the middle of the vast Golden Oasis. It was neutral territory, land owned by neither kingdom. But it was also small and wild, the desert plants so overgrown that not even a helicopter could land there. The bed of the oasis near the shoreline was shifting sand, with water levels that could change overnight, making it dangerous to bring a large boat in to shore for fear of running aground.

"We have palaces the size of football stadiums, mansions in Europe and South America, properties in Asia and Australia, and you want to meet on a patch of sand in the middle of nowhere?" said Ephraim, half laughing.

"The Golden Oasis is not nowhere. It is everywhere," said Darius. "That is the place. Why, are you afraid of the rumors of the peculiar island snakes of Noor Island, vipers and constrictors that eat each other and are always hungry for fresh meat?"

Ephraim laughed. "Snakes and desert islands. What other way to let this twisted tale play itself out, yes? All right, Darius. Noor Island. I am sure Professor Johansen will be thrilled. She is a biologist by training, after all. You, me, and Jan, in a pit of snakes. Let the games begin."

Darius grunted as a vivid image of that night back at Oxford came to mind. But instead of that slim Scandinavian princess between them it was a curvy American queen spread wide and filled deep, from top and bottom, front and behind, inside and outside. He pushed the image away, but the imprint remained, almost like it was a vision of an event that had already happened.

"Noor Island," Darius said, somehow knowing that Ephraim's mind had travelled to the same place in that moment. "The three of us and the snakes. Bring your own anti-venom."

21

"**S**nakes?!" Jan said, both eyebrows raised, both hands on her hips. "A desert island with snakes? What is this, a B-grade horror movie? Will we be staying in a shack that has a shelf full of chainsaws and nail-guns?"

"There is a old guest house on the island, built a hundred years ago. Not a palace, but hardly a shack," said Ephraim. He looked up from the duffel bag he'd been packing and cocked his head. "And why chain-saws?" He pulled out a pronged rod made of brushed aluminum. "A snake-pole is much more effective. Besides, snakes are more afraid of us than we are of them."

"That's so not true. Humans have evolved to no-tice and avoid any movement on the ground. For our ancestors, stepping on a snake was pretty much a death sentence," said Jan, eyeing the snake-pole and shaking her head as she wondered for the millionth time what the hell she was doing here. Was she real-ly about to go on a camping trip with two Arab kings who'd kidnapped her one after the other? Even those ditzy teenagers in the horror flicks weren't this dumb.

She'd spent four days with Ephraim, but after that first savage night of lovemaking she'd stopped him from taking her even when he came at her half-naked, his cock leading the way, erect and heavy. There were a few occasions where she was sure he wouldn't stop, but he stopped every time. It surprised her, actually, because she'd been clearly aroused in his presence, and they'd been close enough to understand that the attraction was there and it was real. But every time she said no, the Sheikh had backed off. Not just that, but he'd held on to his need in a way that made her own need rise: He'd stayed hard, refusing to pleasure himself, refusing to allow anyone else to pleasure him.

And Jan knew there were women in the Royal Palace of Habeetha whose sole function was to pleasure the Sheikh. She'd seen it in the way they looked at her when she passed them in the hallways. They always lowered their heads and covered their faces with their hijabs when in her presence, but they couldn't hide what was in their eyes. Did they love him? Did they hate her? Were they simply worried about losing their jobs?

But Jan had other things to worry about, and it wasn't the harem or the wildlife. Over the past four days Ephraim had showed her the capital city of Habeetha, where almost all the population lived. The streets were smooth and perfect, and the buildings were a wonderful mix of old sandstone bungalows and modern highrises. He'd taken her to the southern division of Habeetha, showed her the grand casino and gambling houses, pointed out the clean, well-lit brothels where well-paid women could safely choose to practice civilization's oldest profession under the protection of the Sheikh's city guard.

As for guards, Jan couldn't help but notice the abundance of uniformed men stationed all over the city, at street corners, in marketplaces, outside mosques and prayer halls, near shopping malls and movie theaters, striding through the streets, patrolling the date-palm lined parks and playgrounds. And then Ephraim took her to the north of the city, to the banks of the Golden Oasis, where his army had their barracks.

"The military cantonment," he said as their gold-plated Range Rover glided through the freshly paved streets lined with young date-palms, past rows of identical sandstone barracks, down toward the shoreline where groups of uniformed young men were being marched and exercised as if in preparation for war. "The result of my biggest mistake as Sheikh."

Jan had stared wide-eyed at the scene, swallowing hard as a chill rose up from the base of her spine. She'd known about the opening of the borders, about the young men flowing in and joining the military to complete their five years of service. But seeing the extent of it was shocking. This was not a simple problem.

"So many men," she said as that chill almost made

her throat seize up. Suddenly she understood the position Ephraim had boxed himself into, and she turned to him wide-eyed. "Wait, how long has it been since you opened the borders?"

"Four years," Ephraim had said grimly.

"So in a year their military service will be done. What happens then?"

Ephraim's jaw set tight as they watched the men march along the banks of the Golden Oasis. "Then I am bound to fulfill my commitment and make them full citizens of Habeetha, give them a stipend, and allow them to live anywhere they choose." He took a long breath. "Some will choose careers in the army, and they will remain here. But these are just barracks, with men living in dormitories. They will all want their own houses, families, lives. And so most will flock to the capital city, and the city center simply cannot absorb so many new people at once. Ya Allah, what a mess I have created!"

Jan thought back to what she'd seen on the tour of Habeetha's capital. The city was clean and beautiful, but it was also small and crowded. Everyone drove expensive cars, but the traffic was heavy despite the wide streets. Sidewalks and marketplaces were busy, and cafés and restaurants seemed to be packed at all hours. There were many tourists, of course—after all, this was the Vegas of Arabia—but that only made everything seem more crowded. Many of the highrises in the city were office buildings or hotels for the tourists, and even without knowing the exact numbers, Jan could tell there was no way the city had enough housing for the thousands of young men who would complete their military service in a year.

"Why not just build more highrises in the city itself?" she'd asked when Ephraim had explained that the desert outside the city was almost impossible to expand into. "If you can't expand the city outwards, then just expand it upwards! Wouldn't that solve any housing problems you might have?"

"The problem is, when you build a highrise, you need to have a foundation that goes very deep into the earth," Ephraim had said. "And the land composition on the fringes of the city simply does not allow for it. The few highrises we have in the city center are already pushing the limits of what we can do." He looked toward the shimmering waters of the Golden Oasis and shook his head. "The only way is that way. Across the shining waters. I know it, Darius knows it, and now you know it."

Jan closed her eyes as her head spun, and she took a deep breath before looking at Ephraim. "OK. But war? An invasion? Shared marriages? Wasn't there some middle ground? What about some agreement for Noramaar to take some of the immigrants?" She'd asked Darius the same question, but she needed to ask it of Ephraim as well.

Ephraim had smiled, his eyes narrowing as he

looked at her. "Do you think Darius can agree? Do you think he will simply tell the people of his kingdom that they will have thousands of new neighbors, military-trained young exiles from the sinful city of Habeetha? And to get my people to move, they would have to be exiled. I would have to force them to move to Noramaar, would I not? After all, many of them were seduced by the freedoms we offer in Habeetha, freedoms that are still against the law in the kingdom of the good Sheikh Darius."

"You keep calling him that," Jan had said. "The good Sheikh Darius. Like you're mocking him or something. What is it with you two? Clearly you know each other, and there is some kind of a strange bond. Yet you exchange public threats and hostilities, and I do believe that you would in fact go to war against him if it came to it. I just don't get it, Ephraim."

The driver of their car turned his head and glanced back at her just then, and Jan frowned when she saw his eyes. She blinked and stayed quiet as Ephraim pressed a button and raised the frosted glass partition between the front and back seats of the custom designed Range Rover.

"What did I say?" she'd whispered when Ephraim turned and grinned at her.

"You called me by my first name without addressing me as Sheikh," he said. "It is considered an insult. I have had people flogged for less."

"You're kidding. You've actually had people whipped

in public for insulting you? Please tell me you're kidding."

"OK, I am kidding," Ephraim had said deadpan, his jaw tight, his eyes narrowing. "Do you feel better now?" He shook his head and smiled. "Ah, Jan. You are still looking at my world with the eyes of an American, a self-proclaimed savior. I may be a king, but I am still a savage, yes?"

"If you're having people flogged in the town square, then yes, you are a savage. I'm not going to apologize for being disgusted by that!"

"An insult to the Sheikh is not an insult to me as a person," Ephraim had explained. "It is an insult to the people of the kingdom. In America you have many symbols that people take pride in: Everything from the great victories of World War II to the dominance of Hollywood to the supremacy in sports and the longest list of Nobel prizewinners. You are a scholar of psychology and biology, Jan. You understand how identity and self-image is fundamental to a person's well-being. In a tiny kingdom, identity and self-image is dictated by the king, Jan. By me! Do you understand? There is a burden of responsibility to display strength and dominance so that my people feel strong, so they may raise their children with pride. Is that not what the people of America take their greatest pride in? Strength and dominance? America dropped two nuclear bombs on Japan, killing millions of men, women, children, and their dogs, cats, and goldfish. Yet the victory in World War II is a source of pride for Americans. Do not misunderstand me—I believe it should be a source of pride for America! What angers me is that you call me a savage for demonstrating strength and dominance in ways that are in line with the peculiarities of my own history and culture."

Jan had taken a long breath and glanced out the window as the car slowly pulled away from the lines of Arab men marching along the banks of the Golden Oasis. Darius had made exactly the same point when he explained why he could never simply make an agreement to open his borders and allow people to flow in from Habeetha. It had to be done in a way that enhanced the perception of him as Sheikh, made him look strong instead of weak, smart instead of foolish. And it was not about the personal ego of a king—though certainly that was part of it—but about what it meant to be king. Which meant that just like Darius would never agree to it, Ephraim could never ask it either! The end result might be the same—a joining of the two kingdoms—but the manner in which it happened was important. The symbolism was important. The symbolism was everything.

And she was the symbol.

That dizzy feeling of being in a made-up world where nothing made sense came back to her when she realized that these two men were in some way prepared to fight their own egos for the good of their kingdoms. After all, what king would step aside and hand the throne to his new queen?! Suddenly it occurred to her that perhaps they were truly reaching for the nobility in themselves, the ability to sacrifice ego for the good of the people while still making sure the perception and symbolism would not affect the self-image of their kingdoms. It was a delicate dance, a careful balance, an operation of great finesse. Oh, God, these men were truly royalty, were they not?

She'd remained quiet for the rest of the journey back to the city center and past the small cluster of highrises as the thought occurred to her that it was by no means settled that anyone was going to give up their thrones. The game was underway, but in a sense it hadn't really begun yet, had it? Who knew what would happen when all three of them came face to face? Setting aside the question of how Darius and Ephraim would react, Jan didn't even know how she would react! She'd shared one passionate night with each Sheikh, and without really talking about it with them, she'd held off from sharing a second night with either of them. Strangely, both Darius and Ephraim had backed off when she asked them to, even though she wouldn't have been able to stop them if they'd advanced and pushed for it. Were all three of them instinctively trying to set a balance, dance this twisted dance of lust and emotion, politics and partnership?

Now it suddenly made sense as Jan watched

Ephraim wave his ridiculous snake-stick as he packed a duffel bag with God-knows-what in preparation for their trip into the unknown. It made sense that they'd chosen this island in the middle of the Golden Oasis. It was symbolic that neither kingdom owned the island, just like neither Sheikh could claim Jan as his own. Their first meeting as a trio needed to be on this one piece of land that symbolized the delicate balance that needed to be struck in order for this to work.

Our first meeting as a trio, Jan thought as she wondered what to even pack. A trio. A threesome. A threesome?

Oh, God, that's what's going to happen here, isn't it, she finally allowed herself to admit as the energy rushed through her in a churn that made her almost throw up. They're both going to take me, one after another, at the same time perhaps. Oh, God, this is my last chance to back out, isn't it. If I agree to go to that island, I'm agreeing to more than just sightseeing, aren't I.

Stop freaking out and think of it as sightseeing, she told herself as she looked at the multiple sets of clean cotton panties she was packing like a good little schoolgirl going to summer camp. You're a scientist and a scholar, and part of the reason you're doing this is to understand and learn, to observe and record, to theorize and experiment.

But it didn't ring true as she felt her body buzz in

a way that made the sickness disappear just as quickly as it had arrived. The truth was the whole scientist-conducting-experiment was a way of tricking herself into taking things this far, a way of telling herself that it made complete logical sense to get involved in this scheme. But now it was time to drop the charade, to push the scientist away and let the human take over. The human woman.

Now's when you learn what it was really like to be a woman a million years ago, shared by the men of the tribe, shared willingly, joyfully, with love and passion and violence and competition all rolled into one. Is that woman inside you? Are you that woman? Can you be that woman?

"We're about to find out," she muttered, smiling to herself and shaking her head as she reached into the travel bag and rifled through the stack of soft cotton panties.

And then Professor Janice Johansen, PhD, grabbed all those panties and quietly took them out of the bag. She was going all in, she decided. Into the unknown. Into the history of womankind. Into herself.

22

"**S**heikh Darius has gone by himself?" Ephraim's driv-er asked again, his dark face twisted by a scowl as he listened over the phone to Darius's attendant, the same woman who had dried Jan's feet on the banks of the Golden Oasis a week earlier. "Ya Allah, Sheikh Ephraim and the American left by boat alone this morning as well!"

Ephraim's driver and Darius's attendant had met several times over the years as part of the entourag-es accompanying the respective Sheikhs when they attended conventions and pan-Arab gatherings of the region's royal families. They'd become friendly, and sometimes spoke when on relief from their du-ties at the same time. This conversation had started as a simple text message from the attendant to the driver, saying that Darius would be away for a few days, visiting Noor Island, and she had time to talk and catch up if he did. The driver had immediately called her with the news that Ephraim and Jan had taken a boat into the Golden Oasis just that morn-ing, with supplies for at least a few days.

"It cannot be a coincidence," the driver rasped,

scratching his thick black beard fiercely as he thought back to the way Jan and the Sheikh had toured the city and talked about policies and politics in a way that seemed odd. After all, she was an outsider, with no business questioning the decisions of the supreme Sheikh of Habeetha! "Not if you say that this same American woman was with Sheikh Darius just last week. Who is she? What spell has she cast over the great Sheikhs?"

"It does not take much for a woman to cast a spell over Sheikh Ephraim, I hear," teased the attendant. "But I admit, it does appear to be a strange coincidence."

"You have heard Sheikh Darius and the American speak," the driver said. "What did they say to each other? You understand English better than I do."

Darius's attendant had remained quiet for a bit. "You know I cannot repeat anything my Sheikh says. It is a betrayal of my position as a personal attendant. Do you not follow the same custom in Habeetha? You do. I know it. How can you ask me to speak of my Sheikh's private conversations?"

"The conversations may be private, but the effects might be public! There is something strange about to take place. I feel it. Four years of the Sheikhs threatening war, and now, out of nowhere, both Sheikhs are having a secret meeting with an American woman who has visited each one privately."

"What are you saying? That she is a spy? A political agent? American CIA? Ya Allah, I promise you, that is not the case," the attendant said, snorting with laughter over the phone.

The driver tensed up and exhaled hard. "Ah, now you have already revealed much. So the relationship between the American and Sheikh Darius is personal. He has taken her to bed? Yes?"

The attendant remained silent, but the driver could hear her breathing quicken in a way that told him he was right. "Sheikh Ephraim has taken the American to bed as well. She has been with both of them in one week. Are you still convinced there is nothing strange in the works? Are you ready to speak of what you heard?"

The attendant stayed quiet for another long moment, but the driver kept going, pushing, cajoling, reminding her that in the end they served their kingdom and not their Sheikhs, that sometimes those in the shadows had to take things into their own hands if they saw something that did not seem right.

"I will tell you what I heard," the attendant finally said, her voice soft but firm. "But only so you understand that what is happening is not a great evil but instead something that could be the greatest good." She paused a moment, as if wondering whether to say what she was about to. "Perhaps then you will see that although it appears that our Sheikhs took this woman to bed, the truth might well be that it was she who took them to bed, that it is she who might be in control, that it is she who we might someday call Sheikha and queen. Queen to both of us, to both our kingdoms."

The driver listened, his disbelief rising with his rage as the attendant spoke of what she'd heard, told of how Darius had ordered a gown of blue silk made for the American, taken her to London to the charity gala where he knew they'd meet Ephraim, of how they'd spoken of shared marriages, symbolism and perception, experiments and traditions.

In stunned silence the driver hung up the phone, not sure if the world had gone mad or if it was just him. He'd gotten used to Sheikh Ephraim challenging tradition by now: After all, gambling and alcohol were banned by Islamic scripture. Still, the driver had seen enough of the hypocrisy of the citizens and rulers of stricter Arab kingdoms, and he knew that thousands of the younger generations openly violated those laws on pleasure trips to the West. So why not expose the hypocrisy and bring it into the light? There was a boldness and strength to Sheikh Ephraim's move that the driver admired, and he also understood that the revenues from tourism would help the country once all the cars in the world ran on electricity and not oil. But this shocking plan to reverse the Islamic tradition of one Sheikh taking many wives was too much. How could that be a show of strength?! It was weakness, to bow to a woman, was it not?! How could Sheikh Ephraim betray the trust and faith of his people like that? It would make all of them look weak and foolish! How could he say with pride that he was a natural-born citizen of the great kingdom of Habeetha once his Sheikh bowed his head to a woman—a brash, rude, unattractive American woman, that too! It could not happen. And it would not happen.

No, he decided as he scratched his beard and clenched his jaw so tight his head hurt. It would not happen.

23

What if it does not happen, Sheikh Darius thought as he pushed open the door to the old guest house on Noor Island. The abandoned sandstone building stood just a few hundred feet away from the banks of the Golden Oasis, and it was in serviceable condition despite being ignored by at least two generations of Sheikhs. The walls, windows, and doors were sturdy, and there was still usable old teakwood furniture: wooden chairs, benches, tables, and bed-frames—though any cloth or cushioning had been removed years ago. The floors were covered with a fine layer of golden sand, but they were clean and with only the faintest of cracks in the sandstone.

Yes, what if it does not happen with the three of us, Darius thought again as he kicked open the door to the inner rooms and stood back, wondering if he would find out about the rumors of snakes the hard way. No movement, and certainly no mythical snakes, and Darius exhaled and wondered again what he was doing here, why he had chosen this place to consummate this plan.

"Because there is no easy way out," he said out loud as he glanced around the empty inner rooms of the guest house and then strode back out to the veranda and stared towards the shimmering waters of the Golden Oasis. He could see his forty-foot boat anchored some distance away, and he could see the dinghy he'd taken bobbing gently where it was tied to an old wooden mooring post. There was no dock or jetty on Noor Island, because the shifting sands beneath the waters changed the levels so much that one could never be certain of the right place to bring a boat ashore. That was part of the reason Noor Island had stayed unused for generations. There had even been a rumor of one of the old Sheikhs being trapped here and starving to death after his boat ran aground. The story was so old even Darius's father could not verify its accuracy, but the rumor was that the entire Sheikh's entourage had been trapped, and when they ran out of food, they began to eat each other.

Just like the snakes, Darius thought as he snorted and tried to ignore the strange anxiety creeping into him as if from behind and beneath. The snakes that I have not seen any sign of, even though the nooks and crannies of an abandoned house would be perfect for them.

As Darius looked out across the waters and contemplated the choices and events that had brought him to an island with invisible snakes and the ghosts of cannibalistic Sheikhs, he saw a black dot on the horizon. It grew larger as he watched, and that anxiety turned to excitement when he saw it was a boat. It flew Ephraim's personal flag, the symbol of the Sheikh of Habeetha. It was him. It was them.

What if it does not happen, he thought for the third and final time as he quickly walked to his bags and unzipped a small black case. He looked inside and took a breath at the sight of two sleek black handguns that lay beside two curved silver daggers. He tried to push away the dread that had taken up residence in him when he realized that if it did not happen between the three of them, he would have to take a different approach to preventing a war. Marriage might be the oldest strategy for preventing war, but it was by no means the only strategy.

24

"What's our strategy here?" Jan asked as she stared at the strange desert plants that grew all the way down to Noor Island's sandy shoreline. "I don't see a dock or jetty, and you've just dropped anchor about a hundred yards away from the island. Are we swimming? So now this is a cross between Jaws and The Cabin in the Woods?"

Ephraim grinned and shook his head, and Jan smiled as she watched the wind play with his long black hair, waving it like a battle flag. "The good Sheikh Darius will come get us, my lady," he said, and there was that mocking undercurrent to the way he called Darius the good Sheikh.

It occurred to her that Ephraim had never answered her question about that, but this wasn't the time to ask, because when she looked out toward the island again she saw Darius.

"Oh, God," she whispered to herself when she saw the taller Sheikh standing on the island, his muscular frame immediately bringing back the memory of how he'd taken her, of how hard he'd made her come.

Then she glanced over at Ephraim, and the memory of how hardhe'd made her come whipped through her mind. "Oh, God, I'm a whore," she muttered as she shook her head. "A stupid whore at that. This is a game, and they're going to rape me, drown me, and head back to their kingdoms laughing like it was all a good joke."

"You said something?" Ephraim asked, turning back towards her from where he was leaning over the front of the boat to make sure the anchor was firmly rooted.

"Just that this is the stupidest thing I've ever done."

Ephraim grinned wider, looking her up and down as she stood there in a black top, a gold head-scarf, a long blue skirt, and pink running shoes that she'd insisted on wearing.

"You mean the stupidest thing you've ever done apart from that outfit?" came the voice, and Jan whipped around to see Darius approaching on his dinghy, smiling wide as he stared up at her, his handsome face throwing her into a state of such utter confusion that she seriously considered diving headfirst into the oasis and swimming in the other direction, fresh-water sharks and man-eating snakes be damned. "Four days with Ephraim, and you are already dressing like a gypsy rebel. What happened to the elegant, sophisticated Professor Johansen with her suit and spectacles? Do you have contact lenses now?"

"Nope. But I'm too afraid to wear my glasses, because then I might see what a mess I've gotten myself into," Jan replied quickly, feeling the tension dissipate almost immediately from the cocky confidence of Darius's quip.

Ephraim grinned as he straightened up and squinted at Darius. It really did seem like these two men were friends—or at least like they could be friends. The energy was strange, surreal, even seductive. She felt herself smiling too, and for one glorious moment, as the sun beamed down on the waters of the Golden Oasis, all three of them were smiling wide.

"Ephraim," said Darius, reaching out his arm as he pulled the dinghy alongside the boat.

"The good Sheikh Darius," said Ephraim, grabbing Darius's arm.

Both Sheikhs wore short sleeves, Darius in white linen and Ephraim wearing black, which seemed to be his color. Jan watched as their brown arms flexed and glistened under the sun, biceps bulging, veins popping as the two Sheikhs held the grip for a long moment, both of them grinning, each Sheikh's green eyes searching the other's face as if looking for some weakness, some way to get the upper hand.

"Getting soft in your old age, I see," Ephraim said when Darius bounded up onto the deck of the boat from his dinghy.

"Better than getting soft in the head," Darius shot back, pulling down the bottom of his shirt, which had crept up to reveal his washboard abs above his low-cut linen trousers.

"This was your idea, I should remind you. Though perhaps I am getting a little soft in the head if I agreed to actually show up here. You know, the logical thing would be to assassinate me right now and take your woman back to civilization where you can live happily ever after," Ephraim said, his smile changing form, eyes narrowing.

"Is that your plan, Ephraim?" Darius said, his own smile transforming as he stood to full height and looked down at Ephraim. "Shall we have it out, then? Guns, knives, or bare hands?"

"Ah, you know me, Darius. I am a man of delicate finesse. Poison in your sweet tea, and then I will watch you sputter and choke while I get a manicure."

"Why don't you two just kiss and get it over with?" Jan said, shaking her head as she watched the back-and-forth between these two Sheikhs. She could feel the tension in the air, but it wasn't an anxious tension. It was the other kind of tension. The good kind. The hot kind. The wet kind.

Both Sheikhs turned to her at the same time, and for a moment Jan wondered if her joke was a bit too much. She thought about what Ephraim had said to her, about how this was a different world, a different culture, with a different history.

But Ephraim just grinned and shrugged. "Ah, if

that was to happen, it would have happened years ago. Right, Darius?"

Darius smiled and ignored the quip. It wasn't that he was bothered by it, Jan could tell. No, it was because his attention had moved from Ephraim to her. And now it was all on her.

"Jan," he said softly as he walked over to her, his green eyes narrowed to such an intense focus that Jan couldn't for the life of her hold the eye contact. "Oh, Jan."

"Darius," she whispered as her insides swirled with emotion, the memories of the passion they'd shared mixing with those moments when she'd stared into Ephraim's eyes as she came, all of it making her unsure of what she felt, of what she wanted, of whom she wanted. "Oh, God, Darius. I . . . don't know what to . . . what to say! I don't know what to do! I just . . ."

"None of us knows what to say," Darius muttered as he came close, so close she could smell his musk once again, the aroma taking her back to that place where the "good" Sheikh Darius had shoved her panties in her mouth and grabbed her by the hair and taken her so hard and deep she swore she could still feel him between her legs. "But I know what to do. Because there is only one thing to do, Jan. Just one thing."

And before she realized what was happening, before she could say another word, he grabbed her by the hair and pulled her head back. Then, with the sun shining down on the waters, with Sheikh Ephraim standing in the background, Darius kissed her full on the mouth. By God he kissed her.

25

Jan wasn't sure if it was the sun blinding her or the feeling of Darius's warm lips on hers, but she couldn't see a thing. She could barely hear beyond the blood pounding in her ears, and if she could speak, it was most certainly gibberish and not a human language.

"Ya Allah, I missed your taste," she heard Darius growl as she felt his tongue push its way into her warm mouth as his strong hands grabbed her ass from behind. He was hard against her crotch, and she could feel her own wetness ooze from between her legs.

Oh, God, I didn't bring any panties, came the thought out of nowhere, and although a part of her wanted to whisper she was a whore and a slut, the thought only aroused her even more. If the last week with each of the two Sheikhs had awakened something in her, then that part of her was more than awake now. It was fully alive and alert. It was taking over.

"You are so wet, my queen," he whispered, and she moaned when she realized Darius's hands were beneath her skirt, the blue cloth hiked up over her ass, his long fingers reaching all the way between her thighs from behind, fingering her cunt from below as his rock-hard erection pressed against her mound. "You are ready for this, yes?"

"I don't know," she muttered as she parted her thighs and almost went limp in his arms as his cock pressed against her stiff clit while he slipped his fingers into her slit and curled them inside her. "I don't know what's happening. I don't know what I'm doing."

"None of us know what we're doing. All we know is that it must be done. Come. Relax, my queen. You are with your king. You are with your Sheikh." A pause, and then Darius spoke again, his voice lower, deeper, darker. "Both your Sheikhs."

Now Jan felt a shadow fall across her, blocking the sun for a moment, and she gasped when she felt two strong hands pull her black top up over her breasts from behind.

"Darius?" she muttered, her eyes still clamped shut, nothing but red stars visible behind her fluttering eyelids. "Darius, what . . . what's happening?"

It took a moment for her to realize that Darius was still kissing her mouth, his hands still beneath her skirt, his fingers still up her pussy. So it was another pair of hands that had pulled up her black top and were now massaging her naked breasts from behind, pinching her pink nipples so hard she groaned and arched her back. And it was another hard cock that was pressing against her ass, another set of lips kissing her neck from behind, biting her earlobes. Another man's smell. Another man's touch. Two men. Two Sheikhs. Two kings.

And one queen.

26

They had stripped her naked before she dared to open her eyes, and when she did she almost passed out from the sight. Darius stood before her, his shirt already off, his trousers unbuttoned and peaked in a way that made her shudder. His body was tight and glistening, the brown ridges of muscle shining in the overhead sun, his green eyes glazed over from arousal as he unbuckled his belt.

She could feel Ephraim behind her, his body pressed so tight against her as he kneaded her breasts that she was almost a part of him, it seemed. She glanced down at herself, gasping when she saw Ephraim's strong hands clamped around her creamy breasts, his thick fingers pinching her erect nipples that were bright red and peaked from how hard and rough he was being with them.

Jan's vision swirled when she looked farther down and saw that her skirt had been pulled off and she was completely naked except for those pink running shoes, and it seemed almost comical, surreal, ridiculous.

Why am I still wearing my shoes, came the thought

as she watched Darius's cock spring into view, its strong upwards curve so pronounced and magnificent that she felt herself release a fresh wave of wetness as if in preparation. Behind her she could feel Ephraim feverishly unbuckling his belt, unbuttoning his trousers, pushing down his underwear until his thick, meaty shaft was rubbing against her naked ass, coating her rear crack with his sticky juice as he growled against her cheek.

"You remember the game, Darius?" Ephraim muttered from behind her. "First one to make her come has the right of first entry."

"What?" Jan muttered as she felt Ephraim step out of his pants and then grab her tight from behind, pulling her down to the smooth wooden deck of the boat. Before she knew it she was leaning against Ephraim's hard body, his strong legs spread wide as her ass nestled against his naked crotch. She looked up and saw Darius standing like a mountain of brown muscle before her, his cock looking enormous as it loomed above her head, a long trail of sticky pre-cum hanging down from its massive red eye.

"You know it is impossible to determine a winner in that game," Darius grunted through clenched teeth, his arousal so vivid that Jan could feel herself salivate as she looked up at his cock that had expanded to the size of a log, it seemed, almost blocking out the goddamn sun.

"Spoken like a loser," Ephraim said, sliding his

hands down past Jan's tender breasts, squeezing her belly, and then massaging her thighs until she spread as far as she could. He fingered her dark lips until she was dripping wantonly onto the smooth wooden planks of the deck, and Jan arched her back and moaned so loud she was sure they'd hear her back in Pittsburgh. "You will not last that long, anyway. She will finish with you and then I will take her like she deserves to be taken. Come, Jan," he whispered as he fingered her with one hand and pulled her head back with the other. "Suck this schoolboy off and then I will take you like a real man takes a woman. Thirty seconds is all it will take, and then it will be just you and I. Come now. Be a good girl and open wide."

Jan's arousal was so strong she couldn't have resisted if she wanted, and she opened her mouth and looked up at Darius. He was so close she could smell the clean musk of his crotch, see the way his heavy balls clenched and released as if he was so close to coming that it was taking all his strength to hold back. The energy between the three of them felt both playful and competitive, and Jan felt herself getting sucked into the game as well.

"Thirty seconds?" she whispered, smiling up at Darius and shrugging against Ephraim's hard body. "That sounds like a challenge for me, doesn't it?"

She heard Ephraim laugh in delight against her, his fingers curling up inside her slit as Darius grinned and stepped right up to her. He slid his fingers through her thick brown hair, holding her head in place, slowly bringing his cock towards her mouth, rubbing his cockhead against her lips until she was coated in his juice.

"If I last thirty seconds," Darius grunted as he slowly pushed himself into her mouth as she groaned and opened wide for him. "Then I get right of first entry."

"So be it," said Ephraim, and Jan heard a beep as the Sheikh set a timer on his watch and then went back to fingering her. "Go."

At the word Darius pushed all the way into her, his massive cock opening her throat so quickly she had to use every ounce of self-control not to gag and pull away. But she managed to hold on, and now she was sucking him, hard and with vigor, his aroma consuming every sense. The feeling of his hardness in her mouth was sublime, and Jan felt a craving to taste him, to feel his heat pour itself down her throat. It was almost a competitive drive that made her suck him like she'd never done for anyone before, and as she heard the timer tick down, she reached up and grasped Darius's heavy balls from beneath and began to massage him, coaxing him to come into her mouth.

"Ya Allah," he groaned as he pumped his cock into her throat, his hands clamping her head so tight she thought her skull would cave in. "I cannot hold it."

Ephraim's fingers were playing an orchestra with

her clit, curling up into her cunt, massaging her outer lips all at once, and the feeling of his cock pressed up against her ass from behind while Darius fucked her mouth was too much for Jan. Suddenly she came, her pussy squirting a blast of juice in a way that almost made her choke on Darius's cock as she wondered if she'd peed all over the deck.

Just then the timer went off, and Darius pulled his cock out of her mouth. Jan's climax hit full force just then, and she screamed up at the sky, spitting out a mouthful of saliva and Darius's pre-cum as she lost control of everything and everyone.

"Oh, God!" she howled, feeling herself being pushed back onto Ephraim's hard body, her legs spreading wide as she felt Darius descend on her from the front.

"She is coming from my touch," growled Ephraim from behind, and Jan felt him reaching between her thighs and buttocks and trying to guide his cock into her slit from beneath. "I have right of first entry."

"Thirty seconds is gone, and I have held my ground," grunted Darius, his voice close to her face, his breath hot against her cheek. "That was the agreement, Ephraim. I am first, and you may follow, like you always do."

Jan's orgasm had hit hard, but now it was rolling back and forth like the gentle waves lapping against the shoreline of Noor Island. She reveled in the swells of ecstasy, and everything around her felt so wet it took her a moment to realize that Darius hadn't actually come and was in fact on his knees as she lay back against Ephraim, his cock pushing into the front of her slit even as Ephraim tried to guide his erection into her from beneath.

For a moment Jan panicked, wondering if these two monsters would tear her apart trying to push themselves into her at the same time, and she flailed and thrashed as she attempted to sit up and get away from them. But Ephraim's grip was tight, and with Darius's weight against her front, she couldn't possibly fight them off. Her panic rose, and she was about to scream for them to stop before a sudden calmness, an almost insane serenity washed over her as her panic settled into a steady buzz of divine arousal.

This is the first test, came the thought as she felt both the Sheikhs' cocks move towards her slit, one from the front, one from behind and beneath. You have to learn how to control these men, balance their power. If you don't, they will indeed rip you apart, rip this whole thing apart. These men are not going to give you their power. You have to claim it for yourself.

"No," she muttered, leaning back against Ephraim and turning her head halfway to receive a savage kiss from him. "I decide, not you. The agreement was thirty seconds, and Darius has the right."

As she said it she slid her ass down against Ephraim, leaning back and spreading her legs so Darius would have full access. She heard Ephraim growl in anger from behind her, his fingers pinching her nipples ferociously as if to punish her. But she would not yield, and she spread for Darius and looked up at him and nodded just she felt his cock line up with the slick center of her vagina.

Darius groaned out loud as he pushed his way into her, and he was so close to coming that after two hard thrusts he exploded into her depths, his entire body tensing up as he released his seed so hard into her she swore she could taste it. Clearly she'd sucked him well, Jan thought as she smiled like a witch while the Sheikh unloaded into her, his strong hips pumping with deep, deliberate thrusts as his cock spurted its semen against the back walls of her cavern.

Darius came for a long time, and Jan smiled the entire way through. Ephraim was still beneath her, his cock hard and full against her soft ass, his fingers still pinching her nipples that were so sore she knew she'd have bruises on her soft breasts by the evening. Finally Darius was done, and with a shuddering groan he pushed out the last of his load and kissed her forehead, her lips, her cheeks, her chin. She kissed him back, still smiling as she relaxed and prepared to be held after the madness of what had just gone down.

And it was only then that it hit her that she wasn't done, not even close.

27

"So you choose to give yourself to him first?! After what we have shared?!" roared Ephraim as he grabbed a fistful of her hair from behind and pulled her away from Darius.

Jan yelped in shock, her eyes opening wide as she was broken out of the wonderful state she'd been in after feeling Sheikh Darius pour the heat of his arousal into her ready depths. She felt Darius's cock slide out of her, and suddenly she was empty, alone, scared as she sensed the fury of Ephraim's unsatisfied arousal.

Oh, God, he's seriously insulted, it hit her when Ephraim whipped her body around to face him, and a chill ran through her when she looked into his eyes. She'd just spent four days with him, and she'd come in his arms as she stared into those eyes. Oh, God, how was she going to manage this?! How could this ever work?!

"You looked into my eyes and came for me," he whispered, leaning close and sniffing her like a dog in heat. "And now you take Darius in your mouth, take him in your cunt, while I hold you like a servant, a slave, a second-place finisher. Never again. Never again. You hear me?"

Jan felt herself nodding as she looked into his eyes, and she smiled and tried to kiss him. But he pushed her face away roughly, even as she tried to kiss him again.

"No," he said. "You do not look at me now. Turn around. On your knees, and turn around. Face the good Sheikh Darius, and let him see you pay the price for giving him first entry."

Jan shuddered as she did what he said. Ephraim was deadly serious, naked and hard as he went up on his knees behind her. His cock was erect and angry, red and oozing, and he gave her one last look before grabbing her hair again and turning her to face away from him.

"Up on your knees for your Sheikh," he ordered, pushing her face forward, angling her ass upwards. "Good. Now look at the good Sheikh Darius, and thank him for what is about to come."

Jan blinked away the haze as fear gave her a clarity that was dazzling. She stared at Darius, who was lazily spread on the deck before her, naked and glistening with sweat, breathing heavily, his cock half-erect and still oozing semen onto the wooden planks. He had a half-smile on his face, and he just looked into her eyes without making any move toward her.

"What's happening, Darius?" Jan whispered as she felt Ephraim's hands leave her for a moment.

"Just look at me," Darius said. "Just look at me. It will be all right after the initial shock."

"Yes, look at him, Jan," came Ephraim's voice from behind. "But do not believe him for a moment. It will most certainly not be all right after the initial shock."

Jan turned her head in panic, and it was just in time to see Ephraim twisting his thick leather belt around his right hand and brandishing it like a whip. Then he smiled at her, looked at Darius for a moment, and without any more hesitation brought the leather tail down smack on her naked buttocks.

She screamed as the whiplash stung her like a thousand needles, and she scrambled to turn away from him. But suddenly Darius was there in front of her, holding her in place, pushing her shoulders down towards the deck so her ass was forced to stay upturned and ready for the next strike.

"What are you doing, you maniacs?!" she screamed as Ephraim brought the whip down on her again, sending shards of pain through her buttocks and thighs. She could see Darius's cock harden before her very eyes, and she strained her neck to look up at him. "Please," she groaned as Ephraim lashed out for the third time, almost making her eyes pop out from the feeling of the heavy leather slapping against her bare, sunbaked skin. "Make him stop."

"Only you can make him stop," said Darius.

"How?" she screamed as Ephraim whipped her again so hard she almost burst into tears. "He's gone mad! How can I make him stop?!"

Darius leaned close, and in his eyes she saw something that made her shiver, like this was another test, a test for him, for her, for all three of them. "Just say stop," he whispered. "If you wish to be queen, act like a queen. You choose. You decide. You command." He took a breath as his jaw tightened. "You choose whether to submit."

Jan stared back at Darius as Ephraim whipped her one last time and then started to spank her bottoms with his open palms, slapping her hard and firm, making her buttocks shiver as he roared. Suddenly Jan decided that she was indeed in control, that even though she couldn't possibly match up with even one of these Sheikhs physically, she was still in control. She thought back to the way she'd looked into Ephraim's eyes as she came for him, and for a moment she understood the perverse rage he must feel at seeing her take another man into her mouth, invite him into her vagina, smile as he came into her depths. They were all being tested, weren't they? It was an experiment for all of them, wasn't it?

So as she felt herself being spanked raw from behind even as Darius's cock began to harden in front of her, Jan smiled and turned her head halfway and whispered to Ephraim: "Don't stop. Let it out, Ephraim. Everything you have. I can take it. I will take it."

As she said it she felt Darius's cock go to full mast in front of her, and without thinking she took him back into her mouth just as she felt Ephraim part her from behind and drive up into her. Suddenly she was filled from front and behind, two Sheikhs taking her at once, sharing her, both of them so hard and monstrous she could barely breathe.

For a moment it felt like time stood still, and she smiled as the sun beat down on her naked back. Her eyes stayed closed, but she could see golden light all around her, like the waters of the Golden Oasis were shining inside her. Then she began to move, slowly, rocking back and forth, acutely aware of Darius in her mouth and Ephraim in her pussy, realizing without a doubt that she was controlling both of them right now, that they were powerless, in her power, that she owned them, ruled them, wanted them, loved them.

A moment later she felt them both come, and her own orgasm rolled in alongside like it had been waiting in the wings, watching Jan's transformation into this woman, this beast, this queen. She swallowed Darius's seed as she clenched her pussy and milked Ephraim's throbbing cock, Darius's balls slapping against her chin as Ephraim's sacks pressed against the fork beneath her ass. Both kings were roaring to the heavens, calling out the name of their god, shouting in Arabic as they shared her sex. But for Jan everything was quiet, serene, calm as the waters of the oasis.

Then as she felt the two Sheikhs finish inside her and pull out, both of them reaching for her stretched and exhausted body as the three of them lay together on the exposed deck, Jan thought that the calm she felt was an illusion, that there was a storm coming, and she was in the eye of it.

28

"We will never see eye to eye on this," said Ephraim, glowering at Darius as the two of them stared at one another across the fire-pit that they'd filled with wood and charcoal that Darius had brought on his boat. "Sex is one thing. But beyond that? It will never be settled."

Darius glanced over toward the door to the guest house. Jan hadn't emerged from inside yet, and the two Sheikhs had been alone for almost an hour. They'd been silent thus far, neither of them wanting to show their hand, to reveal that already they were feeling something for Jan, that this was not going to be as simple as an arrangement that could be managed like a transaction.

"That is why we are here, away from everyone else, just the three of us," Darius said quietly. "Because it has to be settled before we go back. One way or the other, Ephraim. Time is running out, and you know it."

Ephraim took a breath and shook his head. "Ya Allah, I understand why you started this thing in motion. The plan to have two Sheikhs marry one woman is so insane it just could turn this entire mess around and allow us to bring our kingdoms into the future without bloodshed and without shaming our people by either of us looking weak. And it might have even worked if we could manage this as a transaction. But she has gotten to me, Darius. There is something about her, and I do not know if I can share her."

"I worry that I feel the same way. But we must get past it. For the sake of our kingdoms, this is the only way through this. She is the way."

"Kalam farigh," said Ephraim gruffly, running his fingers through his dark hair. "It is not the only way. It is the way you want. You know my army outnumbers yours. You know that if I invade Noramaar, it is by no means certain that Saudi Arabia will come to your aid. You know that you would be forced to surrender or else face casualties that would make your people hate you for sending their sons and daughters to be slaughtered."

"And then what? Those same people would love and respect the victorious Sheikh Ephraim, the man who committed the slaughter? Hah!" Darius clenched his jaw and stared into Ephraim's eyes without blinking. "You cannot threaten me, Ephraim. I know you well enough. If you had the stupidity to attempt an invasion, you would have done it by now."

"How do you know I have not already ordered it,

while you and I are playing this schoolboy's game around a campfire?" Ephraim said, his face lightening a bit as he leaned back and reached for the wine he'd been drinking. "How do you know I will not cut your throat while you sleep? There is no deep hatred between us. In another world we would be great friends. But in this world I would trade your life for the future of my people without hesitation."

"As would I," said Darius, reaching behind him and grasping the leather case he'd carried over from the mainland. "Which is why I have a proposal of last resort. If we cannot get this to work with Jan, cannot manage our own emotions, our own egos, then we work it out the only other way that is right. Man to man. You and me."

He flipped open the case and turned it so Ephraim could see the contents. Ephraim glanced at the two guns and two daggers, and his eyes narrowed and then went wide. He blinked as he glanced up at Darius.

"A duel?" he said slowly. Then he nodded, his green eyes darkening, the flames of the fire dancing in reflection. "A duel," he said firmly, nodding again. "And the winner gets what?"

"Everything," said Darius. "All the spoils. Just like the stories of old. The woman, the kingdoms, everything."

Ephraim laughed, tossing his head back and drinking the wine to the last drop. "Ya Allah, the good

Sheikh Darius! You never cease to surprise me. Join
me or fight me. That is the choice you present, yes?"

"Those appear to be the only two options," Darius said, closing the case with a snap and shrugging.
"I agree, it may not be sustainable to share a woman
that we both might truly care about. Sharing her sex
is one thing. But more than that . . . ya Allah, perhaps
I was wrong. Perhaps even Jan was wrong. Which
means there will only be one real option before war.
We fight it out like kings, just the two of us, putting
ourselves on the line instead of the men and women
of our armies."

The two men sat silent for a while, Darius sipping
his tea, Ephraim drinking his wine. The flames crack-
led and spit as the stars looked down upon them, and
then Ephraim spoke.

"Who will be first husband if we do agree to marry her," he said quietly. "First husband would sit to
her right in the court, be the first to ascend should
anything happen to her. How do we decide that? Another duel?"

Darius laughed, his face settling into a smile as he
glanced at the door to make sure Jan wasn't listening. "There is a way to compete to be first husband.
It occurred to me earlier, when we were sharing her,
making wagers, arguing over the right of first entry."

"Go on," said Ephraim, leaning forward and looking into the flame. "What new game does the good
Sheikh Darius have in mind?"

"The oldest test of a man's strength and power," Darius whispered. "Of a man's vigor, his very essence."

He stayed quiet, watching Ephraim as the younger Sheikh frowned and then opened his eyes wide.

"Ya Allah," said Ephraim. "You are a twisted man, are you not?! Do you mean what I think you mean?"

Darius nodded. "Another sort of duel, but one that ends in life, not death. The first man who gets there is first husband. The first to her womb. The first to get her pregnant. The first to father an heir."

29

Jan listened from behind the door, not sure if she should scream or throw up, run or walk out there and spit in their faces. Her body was now a battlefield, a chessboard, a goddamn playground?! The first to get her pregnant?! Was she living in the Middle Ages?

No, she reminded herself as she took deep breaths to calm herself down. You are living in a world older than the Middle Ages, older than any form of modern society. The world of your ancestors, when small tribes shared everything: food, shelter, mates, and . . . and . . .

Suddenly the answer came to her as she remembered her research into those hunter-gatherer tribes of old who shared it all. Yes, she thought. Perhaps this can work. Perhaps this is the only way it can work. Let them make their move. I have a move too.

Frowning, she walked to the pantry, where they'd laid out all the food and drink. She looked through what she'd brought with her on Ephraim's boat, finally smiling when she found it. A moment later she emerged from the guest house, her hair open and free, her eyes wide and wild, her curves moving elegantly beneath a long silver gown that went down to her ankles and shimmered in the moonlight like flowing water.

"Gentlemen," she said as she tried her best not to turn bright red from the way the two Sheikhs looked at her as she walked past the flames, her ass moving beneath that gown, her breasts hanging free, no underwear on. She'd stopped telling herself that she was a whore, because she knew she didn't believe it.

These men don't believe it either, she told herself when she was greeted with just a tense silence. Jan thought about what she'd heard them say, and it sent a shiver through her when she realized that it was just thin satin that separated her body from these two kings who'd just made an agreement to hand over the right of first husband to the one who got her knocked up first.

But as she looked at their dark, serious faces, each one devastatingly handsome in his own way, each one a true king in his own way, the indignation she'd felt earlier was nowhere to be found. Instead it was admiration—admiration that these men would truly consider giving up their titles to find a way for their kingdoms to merge into one. No matter how twisted the options had become.

"What about two Sheikhs of one kingdom?" she asked as she sat down as gracefully as possible on the wooden bench facing the fire, Ephraim to her left, Darius to her right. She reached for the pot of sweet tea, and slowly poured out a cup. Then she waited a moment and poured out two more, letting them sit before her as the tea cooled. "Didn't you two consider that? Wouldn't that be a way to merge your kingdoms, handle the overflow of Habeetha's population, and still save face and appear wise and powerful to your people?"

Darius glanced at Ephraim and then back at Jan. "A kingdom cannot have two rulers. The ruler marks the identity of a kingdom, sets the tone for his people. Two rulers would be no different than if I simply yielded and opened my borders to make up for Ephraim's folly."

Ephraim grunted, glancing briefly at Darius and then back into the flames. "If you combine two kingdoms, it has to be under one king. One ruler. Darius is right. When two corporations merge, you do not have two CEOs. There are practical considerations for policy and administration, yes, and things run better with one supreme decision-maker. But above it all is the symbolic consideration."

Darius nodded, reaching out as Jan handed him the fresh cup of tea she'd poured. "War or marriage," he said, sipping the tea and smacking his lips. "Those are the only ways two kingdoms can become one. It has never been otherwise."

"And it can never be otherwise," said Ephraim, frowning as he tossed his empty cup of wine to the side and grudgingly accepted Jan's offer of the sweet tea. "The answer lies in war or marriage." He sipped the tea and looked at Jan, his gaze falling to her breasts and back up to her face, glowing in the light of the flickering flames. "And although I would almost certainly win if we went to war, a king's duty must be to prevent war as far as possible. That is the only reason I am even here." He sipped the tea again, his gaze almost a challenge to Jan, as if he meant that he was only doing all of this for his people, not his royal cock. Certainly not for her.

"So why don't you yield to Darius in public," said Jan, taking the first sip of her tea and wincing from the sweetness and aftertaste, half-smiling because she knew the question would irk Ephraim. "Isn't it a show of strength to admit your mistake and ask your neighboring kingdom for help? Isn't that what builds alliances?"

Ephraim snorted, shaking his head and gesturing to Darius, as if to say, "You answer her."

Darius answered, smiling and shaking his head as he explained that if he did that, it would put both of them in weakened positions: Ephraim would look weak for asking; and Darius would still look weak for stepping back and allowing a hundred thousand immigrants to share in his people's land without protest.

Jan smiled and nodded, but in truth she wasn't listening. She already knew the answer to that last question: She'd asked it of both of them before, and she understood the answer. She'd only asked them again to keep them talking, to keep them distracted, to keep them drinking that tea . . .

Now she began to feel the buzz creeping up on her, and she took a deep breath and gulped down the rest of the tea she'd so dutifully poured for all three of them. When she looked up past the flames, she caught Darius staring at her with a glint in his green eyes.

With the hint of a smile and a subtle shake of the head, Darius looked at the cup in his hand, looked back at her, and then gulped down the rest of the tea, wiping his mouth with a silk handkerchief and then tossing the cup aside. By now Ephraim had figured out what was going on too, and he laughed and drank his tea down. Then he stood, and with a flourish he hurled the metal cup far off toward the dark waters of the oasis. He cocked his head and put a hand to his ear as they heard a faint splash.

They all broke into laughter, and Darius clapped his hands and pointed at Jan.

"You," he said, the words slurring a bit, "are not to be underestimated. I was right to choose you."

Jan felt a surreal calm flow through her as the *aruha* she'd mixed into their tea kicked its way into her system. She smiled at the two Sheikhs, and then she slowly shook her head. "You don't choose anymore," she said quietly. "I do. I choose to be queen in public, and I choose to submit to you both in private. I choose."

Ephraim was still on his feet, and he turned and looked down at Jan. She leaned back on the wooden bench, arching out her chest, feeling a sensation of power and confidence surge through her in a way that she was sure wasn't just the drug. It was more. It was her. It was who she was becoming.

"One ruler of two kingdoms, right?" she said, glancing at one Sheikh and then the other. "Isn't that the idea? And how will I balance two kingdoms if I can't balance two kings? This is my training ground, isn't it? This is my training."

She watched as Darius and Ephraim looked at one another and then back toward her. She could feel their eyes glancing at her heavy cleavage in that silver gown, and she leaned back and spread her arms over the backrest of the bench, crossing one leg over the other as her gown rode up to show some thigh. For a moment she felt like a queen, sitting there on her wooden throne, her two knights by her side. Her two knights, her two kings, her two Sheikhs, her two husbands.

She could see their eyes glaze over as they stared at her lips, her bare shoulders, the outline of her nipples beneath the white satin, the curves of her rump and thighs as she sat before them. Perhaps it was the drug, but somehow the thought of two men competing to fill her with their seed was doing something to her.

You already are thinking of yourself as a queen who balances two sides of great power, aren't you, came the wild thought as she watched the Sheikhs shift uncomfortably and glance at each other, each of them adjusting their pants to account for the growing bulges at the front. And you're not going to simply yield to their move, are you? You've got a counter-move, do you not? You're going to match up with them, aren't you? Of course you are.

"I heard what you said," she whispered, slowly uncrossing her legs until she sat plumb in the middle of the long wooden bench, her thighs spread in that satin gown, the cloth gathering around her naked crotch, a gentle wet spot beginning to form. She had her elbows resting on the backrest, her chin pointed up proudly, and she smiled as she spoke. "And I'm fine with it. So let the games begin, your highnesses. Give me your best shot."

The combination of the *aruha* and what she'd just said hit her with a rush of euphoria that made her body light up from the inside, every fiber in her alert and alive. She could see the two Sheikhs visibly harden beneath their trousers, and as each man slowly got to his feet until they faced her, the flames dancing between the three of them, the Golden Oasis silent and dark in the background, Jan reminded herself that if she played this out the way she wanted, this would be no ordinary marriage. She would be playing this game the rest of her life.

Can I do it, she wondered as she watched the flames move while the two kings undressed before her, slowly at first, speeding up as she undid the thin straps of her gown and let her breasts hang free. Can I dance this three-way dance for the rest of my life? A normal marriage thrives on honesty and openness, on being vulnerable and showing understanding, on forgiveness and communication. But this marriage will fail if everyone is honest all the time. Because this isn't just about three people enjoying each other's sex and making sure everyone feels happy and safe at all times—it's about something bigger. Certainly there are already feelings at play here, and certainly I can see myself loving both these men for who they are and what they do to me. But we are all here for politics as much as for pleasure. The pleasure has to be real, but the politics is the reality. If they, as proud and powerful men, are willing to sacrifice their titles and power for the good of their kingdoms, then shouldn't you, as a woman, be ready to sacrifice your conventional notions of what love and honesty in a marriage mean?

And as the Sheikhs stood bare and hard before

her, their dark mastheads glistening in the red light of flame, Jan smiled up at them and nodded. And though the men took it as a signal to descend on her, Ephraim kissing her on the lips ferociously as he grasped her breasts while Darius went to his knees before her open thighs and buried his face in her crotch, Jan knew she was nodding to herself, telling herself yes, she was committing to this all the way, for the rest of her life, whether these men knew it or not.

Whether they knew it or not.

30

Ya Allah, does she know what she is doing, Darius thought as the scent of her sex poured into him as he buried his nose and mouth between her legs, his arousal so strong that he was salivating like a dog in heat. He roughly pulled the thin satin of her gown away, gasping at the sight of her dark triangle of brown curls, her red slit almost glowing in the light of the flames. He took a deep breath of her sex and began to lick her with the flat of his tongue, running up and down her slit lengthwise until she was so wet he could see her juice glistening on her soft, creamy inner thighs.

Above him he could feel Ephraim leaning over and kissing her, pinching and pulling at her breasts. Ephraim was on his knees up on the bench beside Jan as Darius licked her from the ground, and soon Darius could feel Ephraim's fingers down near Jan's crotch as he licked her there.

Jan moaned to the heavens as Ephraim slid two fingers into her even as Darius kept licking her, and Darius knew she was going to come soon, come hard, come for them. For both of them.

Suddenly it hit Darius that Jan had heard them and she was fine with it?! What did that mean? Was she truly prepared to choose whichever Sheikh's seed rested in her womb first? Did she see no difference between Darius and Ephraim? Were the two of them simply tools, machines, beasts of burden to give this queen what she wants?

The thoughts were mad, and Darius tried to remind himself that he was on a drug. But the thoughts kept coming as he tasted her from the inside, driving his tongue into her vagina as he felt Ephraim rub her clit roughly and pull at her matted pubic hair as he fingered her. Jan was moaning loudly, writhing in their arms, her soft thighs closing and opening wildly against his face. He glanced up for a moment and saw Ephraim holding her throat as he kissed her, still fingering her with the other hand, and from the way Jan's buttocks were shuddering from the tongue and fingers inside her, Darius knew she was about to come.

He kept going, pushing his face deeper into her crotch as his erection surged to full hard. Darius wanted to take her now, hard and deep. He wanted to fill her like he'd done on the plane that first time, on the boat earlier that day. How many times had Ephraim fucked her, he wondered as a momentary rush of anger blasted through him. Suddenly he couldn't breathe, and he pulled his face away from between

Jan's legs, his eyes going wide as he raised his head and stared up at Ephraim kissing her hard, biting her lips, licking her cheeks as she moaned and shuddered. She was already starting to come, her moans turning to wails as her orgasm came screaming in while Ephraim curled his fingers up in her, rubbing her clit furiously with the butt of his thumb.

Darius sat there on his haunches, taking deep gulps of air as he stared at his rival kiss and finger his woman, his queen, the one he'd chosen. Did she even care who was fucking her? Did she even notice he'd backed away? Did she even—

"Darius," she moaned suddenly, her eyelids fluttering as she tried to focus, one hand reaching out into empty space, her fingers clawing desperately at nothing as she tried to reach for him. "Where are you? Don't stop. Please."

Her need was real, and Darius's cock flexed involuntarily at the sound of her plea. Ephraim turned and looked at Darius for a moment, and Darius saw that same flash of anger in Ephraim's peaked face, that same mix of jealousy and competition. Ephraim was naked too, his cock flexing hard as their queen called for Darius. It made Darius almost laugh in delight, because now he could feel that wild, manic, almost violent arousal that he instinctively understood only came to be when a man was competing for a woman at the most primal, fundamental, physical level.

Through the throes of his ecstasy and the madness of the *aruha*, it really seemed like the presence of another hard cock was making him want her more, need her more, lust for her in a way that might never happen with just one-on-one sex.

It is that primal sense of competition, the need to make sure that it is indeed my seed that makes it to her womb first, Darius decided as he grinned at Ephraim and then spread Jan's thighs and pushed his face against her wet crotch again. Both Ephraim and I feel it, and it is like a drug in itself, yes?

Jan kept coming as the thoughts flowed through Darius's head, and he could feel her fingers clawing at his thick hair, he could taste her juices flowing down the corners of his mouth, he could smell her sex so strong and clean that it was all he could do to clench his balls and not come all over the sandy ground of Noor Island.

Finally Jan pushed his head away and clamped her thighs shut tight as she shuddered through the death throes of her orgasm, and Darius pulled back and sat down on his naked ass. Ephraim still had his hand around her throat, and he was hard and throbbing, clearly trying to push her onto her back so he could enter her.

"No," she whimpered. "I need a moment. Stop. Stop!"

Ephraim growled like an animal, and Darius tensed

up when he saw Ephraim's hand tighten around her throat. Jan opened her eyes and locked her gaze with Ephraim's, and he growled again and tried to stare her down. They stayed like that for a long moment, Ephraim's right hand tight on her throat, the head of his cock touching her naked belly, his left hand holding her breast, fingers pinching her nipple so tight it was white from the pressure.

Darius fought the impulse to stand and pull Ephraim away from Jan, throw him to the ground, kick him in the face, do whatever he needed to do to get him away from Jan. Is it because I want to protect Jan, or simply because I want to do to Jan what he is about to do, he wondered as he watched the two of them look into each other's eyes before Ephraim slowly released her throat and stood down, grinning wide and nodding as he did it.

"As you wish, your highness," Ephraim whispered, leaning forward and licking her cheek before backing away. He looked down at her naked body, creamy white and shining in the firelight. Then he glanced at Darius, grinning again when he saw how hard and ready they both were. "But I have right of first entry this time. Remember that."

Darius smiled tightly, glancing at Jan and then back at Ephraim. "And you must remember that it is I who chose Jan, it is I who brought her to us, it is I who chose to share her with you." His smile vanished when Ephraim turned to him and locked eyes. "And so it is I who will always have right of first entry."

Ephraim held the gaze, and Darius could feel the heat build as the fire flickered and danced in the background. Finally Ephraim broke a grin, shrugging his powerful shoulders and standing up off the bench, shaking his head as he started to laugh. "No matter," he said, walking over to the steel wine flask sitting on the sand. He took a long swig and shrugged again. "You can have right of first entry. It will not last long. Once she is with my child, first right will be mine."

"Says who?" came Jan's voice, cutting through the tension as both Sheikhs turned to her and stared.

"That is tradition," said Ephraim, frowning deep, his eyes narrowing. "When a Sheikh takes four wives, the first wife always has pride of place. In the court, at the dinner table, and in bed. We made an agreement."

Jan shook her head, smiling as she looked at Ephraim and then at Darius. "The two of you made an agreement, and so it stays between the two of you. You guys want to put your sperm in competition, go ahead. You guys want to agree that the winner—whatever that means—gets pride of place in the queen's court? Great. I do understand that I'm not going to be some dictator ruling your kingdoms, that I'll be a figurehead to a large extent, that the two of you will always be behind me, ruling your kingdoms through me. I'll be ruling on your behalf, and I wouldn't have it otherwise. I wouldn't be able to do it on my own—it's going to take me years to even become fluent in Arabic, for God's sake. I understand that this is about perception and finding a way to combine your kingdoms without war and without making it look like either of you has compromised or yielded. So yes, I understand that the two of you will control how your kingdom is run, and I'm on board with that. It's your right. But when it comes to my body . . . well, those rights are mine and mine alone. I decide now, and I will decide then."

"The father to the heir will be first husband," said Ephraim, shaking his head. "It cannot be otherwise."

"He is right, Jan," said Darius. "There are precedents. History. The way things are done."

Jan smiled, her brown eyes shining in the light of the fire, her skin glowing from the sweat and heat generated by their three bodies. They were all naked, sitting by the fire, beneath the stars, the angels and devils of the Golden Oasis watching them.

"All right," she said slowly, glancing at Ephraim and then Darius. "All right. First to father an heir is first husband. Are we happy now?"

"We are happy," said Ephraim with a grin. He glanced at Darius and then down at his cock, which was still hard and heavy. "Though only one of us will be happy when the inevitable takes place and my seed proves to be the stronger."

Darius grinned back at him, and his cock stiffened at the call to compete, the energy surging through his hard frame as if a million years of evolution was spurring him forward, reminding his body that the history of man can be boiled down to the simple contest of one man's sperm against another's.

Darius stood to full height, and he saw the way Jan gasped when she glanced at his thick cock, his heavy balls, his broad chest, flat stomach. She is yours, came the thought from that ancient part of himself. Yours, and perhaps yours alone.

"She is mine first," came Ephraim's rumble from his left, and Darius glanced over to see the younger Sheikh on his feet too, facing not Jan but Darius himself. For a moment the two kings stared at each other, their cocks erect and angry, balls heavy and ready, green eyes glazed with the madness of the drug, the craze of lust, the fire of pride.

Time stood still as the two naked beasts stood illuminated by the dancing flames, and from the corner of his eye Darius thought he could see shadows moving in the dark desert plants beyond their circle of light. Imagination? Hallucination? The snakes of myth? The ghosts of lore?

This is our Garden of Eden, is it not, Darius thought as he looked into Ephraim's eyes and swore he saw the devil, the Shaitaan himself. Or perhaps I am the devil, came the thought as he caught the image of Jan sitting naked on the bench watching them, a half-smile on her face. There were three players in the Garden of Eden, yes? Adam, Eve, and the devil. And there are three players in this story, yes? So if she is Eve, which one of us is Adam and which one the devil?

The thoughts almost drove him insane as he stayed locked in on Ephraim. The Old Testament and the Quran shared the same stories, the same characters, the same players, and all of it spun together and ripped apart as those shadows danced and clapped in the background. Have we both taken a bite of the apple, tasted the forbidden fruit, begun our descent, our fall from grace, he wondered as he saw Ephraim lean his head back and roar with laughter. Jan was laughing in the background too, their sounds of mirth coming through to Darius in waves, the ripples taunting him, exciting him, terrifying him.

He thought of that case with the guns and knives, wondering if that was the only sane course of action at this point. Was he really going to hand over his throne to a woman he'd known a few weeks? Was he really going to share his kingdom with a beast like Ephraim? Was he really going to send his small army to be slaughtered in battle with Ephraim's hordes if they invaded? No. How could he do any of that? The only sane option would be to end it here, to end it now. To end Ephraim. To take one life for the good of millions. It was the way of a king. The way of a leader. The way of a Sheikh.

He blinked and cocked his head as the visions grew

stronger, and although Darius knew it was the *aru-ha* affecting his judgment, he could not break his thoughts away. It seemed so simple. Why twist and turn your way to a solution when the answer can be arrived at directly, with one bullet or a single slash to the throat? Is that any less insane than the situation you have already engineered? Do it, Darius! Do it!

The Sheikh half-turned as he swore he heard the words whispered as if from outside himself. The dark bushes beyond the fire seemed to be moving, and Jan's laughter was piercing and shrill. Too shrill.

Suddenly he realized Jan wasn't laughing at all. She was screaming! The realization came to Darius slowly, and he turned as if in a dream to see where Jan was pointing. Then he saw it: There on the ground, slithering and shining, gold and black, long and twisted.

Ephraim was still laughing when the snake approached him, and everything seemed to move in slow motion as Darius watched the viper's fangs emerge and sink into the brown flesh of Ephraim's calf.

Perhaps you will not need to do anything at all, came the thought from the darkest reaches of Darius's mind as he watched Ephraim's laughter fade, his expression changing to one of confusion as the snake's poison entered his system. Perhaps this is fate, destiny, Allah deciding who is the true ruler of these lands, the true Sheikh of the Golden Oasis. Do nothing, Darius. Let fate take its course.

Darius stared as Ephraim sank to his knees, naked and bronze, his green eyes clouding over as he clutched his calf. The snake was gone, its tail disappearing into the bushes as Darius wondered if all of it was an hallucination brought on by the *aruha*.

Jan's screams were still shrill in his head, and she was saying something that for the life of him Darius couldn't interpret. His eyes were locked on Ephraim, his rival, his enemy, his . . . his co-husband? His partner in marriage? His brother? His friend? His family?

You decide, came the whisper on the warm desert breeze that drifted in from over the dark waters of the oasis. You started this, and you can decide how it ends. You can decide if you follow through or back out, if he is your enemy or your family, if he is Adam and you are the devil.

Perhaps we are both the devil, he wondered as he saw Jan scream again and then get up and run toward the guesthouse, still saying something he couldn't understand because of the blood pounding in his temples. Or perhaps we are both Adams, the first men in the story, a new story, a new epic, a new way. You decide, Darius. You decide.

And as if spurred by something beyond logic and sense, Darius felt himself step forward, toward Ephraim, his fallen enemy. He reached down and grabbed Ephraim's hand by the wrist, pulling it away from the wound as Ephraim tried to hold it there.

Let the poison run through his veins and stop his heart, came that whisper from the devil inside, the devil that lives inside every man, whispering at times of crisis, offering an easy way out of every hard choice, reaching out a gnarled hand to pull man from his eternal state of grace.

"No," rasped Ephraim, his eyes red and wild as he stared up at Darius. "What are you doing?!"

"Let go," said Darius. "Let go, brother. It will be all right."

Ephraim looked confused and scared, and for a moment Darius felt like an older brother. A warmth poured into him as he smiled and looked deep into Ephraim's eyes. Then Darius took a breath, and without any more hesitation, went down on his knees, put his mouth over the snake's fang-marks, and sucked out the poison just as Jan came racing back out of the guesthouse with the antivenom.

31

Ephraim's vision had narrowed to the point where he could barely see his own hand clutching the wound. He knew he'd been bitten, but there was no pain. He knew the poison would be entering his system and making its way to his nervous system and heart, but he remained calm even as he fell to the ground and lay there naked in the sand. Perhaps it was the factual knowledge that remaining calm slowed his heartbeat, which in turn made the poison move slower. Or perhaps it was another kind of knowledge, a sense that this was another test, another trial, a twisted version of that first test of man in the Garden of Eden.

"No," he'd whispered as he watched Darius approach, the older Sheikh's green eyes looking bright and wild from the flames that seemed to have risen higher even though Ephraim didn't remember either of them adding any wood to the fire. "What are you doing, Darius?"

He'd known that Jan must have raced to the guesthouse to grab the anti-venom that she'd insisted on bringing after he told her the stories of snakes on

Noor Island, and he knew he just had to remain calm and wait for her to save him. What in Allah's name was Darius doing? Was he trying to release the pressure on the wound so the poison would move through his system faster and kill him before the anti-venom got there? Was he trying to end this game by doubling down on what fate had thrown at them?

Perhaps this is our destiny, came the thought as Ephraim felt his hand being pulled away. Perhaps I die here, my spirit joining with those that live in the shadows of Noor Island. Perhaps Darius is the evil Sheikh in this story after all. He'd grinned as he thought that, looking into Darius's eyes again as he watched him bend down. Or perhaps we are both the evil Sheikhs, both of us fallen forever, this plan of ours the cause of our downfall. Perhaps it is Allah and the angels forsaking us, punishing us, condemning us.

Suddenly Ephraim felt the clarity of pain, and he gasped when he saw Darius's mouth close over the fang-marks. He felt the suction as Darius pulled the poison out of Ephraim's body and into his own, and he watched as Darius spat into the sand and then repeated the action, again and again, cleansing him, cleansing both of them perhaps.

Then Jan was there with the anti-venom, and some long, tense moments later the three of them were huddled together, naked and without shame, just like in that magical garden before the fall.

We have not fallen, came the thought as Ephraim felt his head being cradled in Jan's soft lap even as Darius's strong hands tied a tourniquet just above the wound to make sure the last traces of poison didn't make their way up his bloodstream. No, we have not fallen but instead have risen. We have risen, and we will keep rising into this new world that we are creating, this new kingdom of man that will be blessed by Allah and the angels. We have risen together, the three of us. We have risen.

32

The sun rose slowly as Jan caressed Ephraim's thick hair and touched his forehead. The fever was gone, and she exhaled as she glanced down at his leg and then over at Darius, who was seated on the ground alongside, dreamily gazing toward the eastern horizon.

"You'll go blind if you stare at the sun," she said softly to Darius as she ruffled Ephraim's hair. "Didn't your mother ever warn you about that?"

Darius lazily glanced over at her. "I never knew my mother." He paused for a moment, looking down at Ephraim, who was awake and alert and seemed to be thoroughly enjoying the attention he'd been getting over the past two hours as Jan and Darius anxiously waited for his fever to subside. "Neither did he."

"You are correct," said Ephraim, moving his head on Jan's lap and grinning at Darius. "I did not know your mother."

Darius laughed and shook his head. "Ya Allah, that poison seems to have made you sharper. Perhaps we should all take a swig of it." Then he took a breath and gazed meaningfully at Ephraim before looking up at Jan. "I mean of course that neither of us knew our mothers. Both Ephraim and I were born at great cost."

Jan felt Ephraim's body tense up as he lay against her, and she pulled her hand away from his hair so he could sit up. She frowned as she looked at Darius. "You mean both of your mothers died in childbirth? That's a weird coincidence."

"Coincidence is one way of putting it," said Ephraim, sitting up and pulling his knees up to his chest as he examined the dressing Jan had put on his snakebite. Then he glanced at Darius. "Shared curse is another way."

"Well," said Jan, blinking as she tried to make light of the sudden heaviness in the air. "I know my mother all too well, and that isn't always a blessing, let me tell you guys." She paused. "What about your fathers," she asked quietly, looking at Ephraim and then Darius. "There isn't a lot of detail on the Internet about you guys or your kingdoms—at least not in English. I tried using some online translation tool to read a few Arabic sites, but the results were too messy to get a clear picture. All I know is that you're each an only child." She paused again. "Whose mothers both died in childbirth, it appears. So what about your fathers? They were the Sheikhs before each of you took over, yes?"

Darius grinned and shook his head, glancing at Jan and then at Ephraim, green eyes shining in the rising sun. "Do you want to tell her or should I?"

Ephraim grunted. "Go ahead. This whole thing was

your idea to begin with. Tell her. Tell her that both our kingdoms were ruled by Sheikhas, not Sheikhs. That our mothers were both queens, each of them the only children of the previous generation."

Darius rapped his knuckles against Ephraim's dressing, making the younger Sheikh wince. "I thought I was going to tell the story. Next time do not steal my thunder, Ephraim." He grinned and then glanced over at Jan, nodding his head. "Yes. Our fathers were both outsiders, brought into the kingdoms by marriage. It was our mothers who were the heirs, the rulers, the queens."

Jan frowned, blinking hard as she glanced at one Sheikh and then the other. They'd both mentioned their days at Oxford, and indeed they'd both referred to being kings back then. Kings, not princes. "Wait, so after your mothers died, the thrones of Habeetha and Noramaar passed directly to each of you? Not to your fathers?"

Darius nodded, his brown muscles flexing. All three of them were still bare-skinned, sitting close together by the fire, which was somehow still going as the sun rose over the waters of the oasis. The breeze was warm and gentle against Jan's skin, and perhaps it was still the *aruha* in her system, but she didn't feel an iota of self-consciousness as she sat with her two naked kings on a blanket.

Ephraim nodded. "There were councils and proxies in charge until we came of age, of course. But yes—I was twelve when I ascended to the throne of Habeetha. Darius was ten when he first wore the crown of Noramaar."

"Wow," said Jan. "That's young. So your fathers ruled on your behalf until you came of age?"

Darius shook his head. "No, just the councils. Our fathers had no standing by our laws. They were both outsiders. They had both married into the royal families of Habeetha and Noramaar."

"Did they have other wives?" Jan asked, frowning again as the strange parallels between the two Sheikhs' lives began to emerge.

"No," said Ephraim. "The husband of a Sheikha is not permitted to take other wives according to the laws of both our kingdoms. An unusual rule, but not unheard of. Still, it caused some distress in our fathers' family, if the stories are true."

"Both our fathers were cut off from their own family for choosing to marry our mothers," said Darius. "It was considered an act of submission and weakness for them to forsake the right of a man to take multiple wives."

"Were they from royal families too?" said Jan.

Darius nodded and took a breath. "Yes." He stayed silent, and Jan felt a strange unease as she watched Ephraim glance over at Darius and then look toward the fire, whose flames were finally getting drowned by the gold of sunlight.

"Family," said Ephraim quietly, his jaw tight, his

eyes narrowed, his expression confusing Jan for a moment.

"Family," she repeated, still confused at why he'd said the word. And then it hit her. Both Sheikhs had used the word "family," not "families" when talking about their fathers' origins. "Wait," she blurted out, her eyes going wide. "Your fathers were from the same family? Your fathers were related?"

"Brothers," Darius said, his voice barely a whisper, his eyes narrowed into slits as he stared at the flames along with Ephraim. "Two brothers who walked away from their kingdom and family. Two brothers who bowed their heads to their wives and queens, took on background roles in new kingdoms, an act that back then would mean ridicule and shame for the family."

"Why?" said Jan, not sure what she was asking, for the moment ignoring the revelation that these two men were in fact cousins. Somehow that didn't shock her as much as it should have. It seemed to explain that underlying bond they seemed to share even though they were at one another's throats in the press. If anything, that was the mystery now: How could Ephraim and Darius, knowing that they shared the same blood, be at one another's throats and on the brink of war?! Yes, certainly the history of the world proved time and again that brothers killed brothers, sons murdered fathers, and mothers poisoned their daughters for wealth, power, and politics. But Jan was certain there was something more here.

Why had they never mentioned being cousins? Why had there been nothing in the local news about their connection? What was she missing?

"Why?" she asked again, not sure which question she was asking first. "Why doesn't everyone know about this? Shouldn't this be a major part of the press coverage of your feud?"

Ephraim grunted, touching his dressing again and shrugging. "Our mothers died over thirty years ago, Jan. And they had us quite late in life, which means their own marriages took place forty or so years in the past. Before the Internet. Before the time when everyone knew everything about one another."

"Back then a royal family could closely guard its secrets, control what information made it outside the family and the kingdom," Darius added, squinting toward the sun and then reaching for his sunglasses. He put them on, looking almost comical: A lean, muscled, bronze Adonis, naked except for his Porsche Design sunglasses. He grinned and shrugged, and for a moment Jan thought his broad shoulders moved in the same way Ephraim's had when he'd shrugged earlier. "Our fathers were young when they married our mothers, and they were written out of the family history, lineage, and fortune. In a sense they did not exist as anything other than the husbands of Sheikhas. It was done to insult them as much as anything. To strip them of their identity."

"And did it?" Jan asked softly, her head spinning

as she tried to understand the patterns being played out here, if perhaps this part of their shared history was why these two proud Sheikhs were willing to experiment with this radical arrangement. Were they trying to make up for something? Prove something? Reclaim something? Fight something in themselves? Accept something? Reject something else? Who the hell knew?! Oh, God, why didn't she study psychology instead of sex?!

But perhaps the sex has brought you to the answer, came the thought as she watched her naked kings relax as the sun warmed their naked frames, both of them smiling now as they talked freely about secrets that perhaps they had never talked about, perhaps never even thought about this explicitly! These men have sought you out for all those reasons, she thought. The psychology is complex, just like a person's identity is a composite of experience, genetics, upbringing, actions of intent, events of accident. Look at how these men are talking about their past now, freely and openly, exposed and honest like their bodies under the morning sun. Would this have ever happened if not for what these bodies have shared?

And what have these bodies shared, Jan? What have they shared?

You, came the answer on the breeze that rolled in off the surface of the Golden Oasis. They've shared you.

Jan gazed at the two naked Sheikhs as that warm breeze enveloped her even as the sun bathed her in golden heat. Neither of them had taken a bride, and as far as she could tell, neither of them had even come close to it. By now she knew of Ephraim's history with his harem, and she'd read snippets of press talking of a younger Darius with models and actresses, but there'd never been any serious links, no broken engagements, nothing even close. Why? It had to be related to the strange connections between their fathers, the way those old marriages had stripped those men of their identity and history, made them nothing more than husbands of queens. Were these two men secretly afraid that taking brides would do the same to them? Was that why they were subconsciously prepared to share her—because they felt that between the two of them they could control her, possess her, dominate her, own her?

"You're scared," she blurted out, her thoughts completing themselves in speech as the two Sheikhs stopped mid-sentence and turned toward Jan. "You're both terrified that what happened to your fathers will happen to you, that marrying a woman somehow takes away your power, your identity, your independence. That's it, isn't it? That's part of this, whether you two can admit it or not."

Ephraim's face clouded over as he stared at Jan, and although Darius's eyes showed a glimmer of recognition, he stayed silent too. Then Darius took a breath and glanced at Ephraim.

"I will admit it if you admit it," he said, half-grinning though something in his voice told Jan that she'd hit home—at least for Darius, who was clearly the more self-aware of the two Sheikhs.

"I admit nothing," Ephraim said quickly, not even a half-smile showing on his dark face. "My identity does not depend on a woman, and it never will." He looked back at Darius. "And if yours does, then you are weak, Darius."

Darius smiled, not taking the bait, his own green eyes narrowing as he stared down the younger Ephraim. "Marriage is about sharing an identity, merging identities with another, creating a new identity from the union. You know that, Ephraim. That is why, just like me, you have never married or even come close to it. You know, just like I do, that marriage will change some part of your identity." He glanced at Jan, then down at himself, and finally back at Ephraim. "It will change all of our identities. It cannot be otherwise."

Ephraim shook his head, the darkness in his eyes more pronounced as he stared at the ground. "I do not yield my identity to anyone. I would not even consider it."

"But you are considering it. You are here, and that says everything," said Darius without missing a beat, and Jan's breath caught as she saw how Darius was taking control of the conversation without losing his cool.

"All it says is that I am a gambler and a player of games," Ephraim replied. "That is my identity, and no woman . . ." he paused and glanced at Jan, blinking and then looking away, ". . . no matter who she is, will make me submit. No woman will make me yield."

Jan could see that Ephraim wasn't going to yield to any argument, submit to any logic, nod his head and agree with any point Darius made, no matter how reasonable or obvious. He was too stubborn, much more so than Darius, and certainly less willing to accept the vulnerability in himself. He needed to be shown that Jan wasn't asking either of them to submit to her. She didn't want that, and she knew it. Not in private, at least. Not when it was the three of them. She'd already submitted to each of them in private. She'd already submitted to both of them together in private. Now it was time to take it a step deeper, a step farther, a step darker. It was time to see if they could submit—not to her, but to each other. After all, this marriage would be three way, and since both men were clearly heterosexual to the point where they were not in the least threatened by being around one another's naked bodies, Jan knew she'd always be between them, the connection, the shared space, the conduit to this new shared identity that would need to happen before their kingdoms could ever be joined.

Which meant Ephraim needed to be shown that Darius was right about marriage being a commitment to creating a new shared identity, a merging, a union. But Darius needed to be shown something too: that the new identity would only come about as a result of action, not words. Action and experience. And experience was the realm of the body, was it not?

Yes. It was time to move from the realm of words to action once again. But what action? How to bring Ephraim around? How to make him yield by showing him that he would never have to yield at all?! And how to make Darius see that although he had been the first and in a sense would always be the first, he would need to yield to Ephraim too, make way for his co-husband. Make way for Ephraim . . .

Oh, God, she thought as the answer came from the core of her body, making her shudder even though the sun was hot and bright above the three of them. Oh, God, can I do that?

"No," Jan said, her voice trembling when she realized what had just gone through her mind. "No one is going to make you yield, Ephraim." She glanced at Darius and then back at Ephraim. "In fact, I am going to ask Darius to yield." She took a breath and blinked as Darius's face clouded over with a deep frown. "I'm going to ask him to yield first rights to you, Ephraim."

"First rights will be determined by whose child you bear first," growled Darius, shaking his head, still frowning as if he was trying hard to understand what the hell she was playing at. "We have already agreed on that."

"I'm not talking about the right of first husband. We'll cross that bridge when we get to it. Right now there's another bridge to cross . . ." Jan whispered, slowly standing up, not missing the way both Sheikhs' cocks moved as she stood there naked before them, her breasts hanging free, her legs firmly together, her dainty triangle looking like dark-brushed gold in the sun as the warm breeze swirled around her naked buttocks, whispering for her to go forth, to go on, to go where she'd never gone before—where no man had ever gone before.

Slowly she walked past the kings and back into the guest house. She found her bag and rummaged through it to find the little jar of virgin coconut oil she'd carried with her. With trembling fingers she opened it and touched the clean, natural lubricant, taking a deep breath and blinking hard before turning and walking back toward the door leading out to where her Sheikhs were waiting.

Silently Jan placed the jar of lubricant on the thick blanket between the two Sheikhs, and then she slowly went down on her knees. Her heart was pounding, her breathing getting heavy as her heat rose even as she saw Darius's cock filling out in a way that told her the older Sheikh understood.

He may understand what I'm suggesting, but will he accept, Jan wondered as she slowly leaned forward onto her elbows, raising her rear as she heard Ephraim mutter in Arabic and sit up straight, his cock hardening so fast Jan almost gasped.

"Darius was the first to have me," Jan whispered as that tingle whipped through her core once more when she realized both Sheikhs were fully hard again, rising to their knees behind her, Ephraim stroking his cock as Darius's erection flexed on its own, the tension mounting as they once again got pulled into the competition of who would mount her first, a competition that she knew would last their entire lives, giving her an excitement that would always make her wet and breathless because of the way it touched a hidden part in her psyche, perhaps her soul. "Nothing can change that. But perhaps we can balance it out." She turned her head and glanced at Darius, into his green eyes. She was getting to know these men better now, and another shiver passed through her when she allowed herself to admit that perhaps she could truly love both of them, truly bond with each of them as individuals, truly see herself as the wife of two men.

But first the three of us have to strengthen our bond, she told herself. The competition between them when it comes to my sex is arousing and exhilarating, and clearly it gets them going as well. But along with that there needs to be cooperation, a true sharing of my sex, a real balancing of these men's needs.

"Darius," she whispered as she held his gaze for a long moment and then glanced quickly at the jar of clear oil. "Are you ready to truly share me with him? Are you prepared? Really and truly prepared?"

Darius moved forward on his knees, his jaw tight, his muscular thighs flexed and thick as his heavy cock bounced gently, its shaft so thick that Jan almost choked in fear when she remembered that Ephraim was even thicker! Can I do this, she wondered as she felt Darius's hand caress her smooth white buttocks as Ephraim growled in the background like a goddamn animal ready to fight. Can I take this?

"I do not need his permission," Ephraim said as he moved forward from her left, caressing her thighs from behind as Darius massaged her ass. Ephraim's fingers moved up from beneath slowly, and Jan could feel her pussy respond with a release of warm wetness as two pairs of hands massaged and rubbed her ass and thighs from behind, their strong fingers kneading and pressing with increasing force until they were massaging the lips of her vagina together from beneath, fingering her until she could barely speak as her juice dripped onto their hands and fingers, her aroma filling the air.

"I asked Darius a question, and I want both of us to await his response," Jan muttered, trying her damnedest to stay in control as she felt so many fingers enter her that she almost came right there, on all fours in the dirt, like a goddamn animal. She turned her head halfway and glanced at Darius, whose face was peaked with arousal. "Are you prepared to share me, Darius?" she asked again, turning her eyes to the innocent white jar of oil on the blanket and then looking back into his green embers that were ablaze with both recognition and conflict.

Slowly Darius's hands moved away from beneath her open thighs, up along her sides, grasping her buttocks firmly as Ephraim continued to rub her clit and mound. Then Darius parted her rear crack with his strong hands, and Jan almost fainted when she realized that both Sheikhs were silent and hard, Ephraim to her left, Darius right behind her, both men staring at her clean, dark rear, her most forbidden space, her most virgin place.

"Yes," Darius whispered as he leaned forward and kissed her rear pucker in a way that almost made Jan choke with the most filthy arousal as she struggled to stay conscious enough to control what was going to happen. "Yes, I am prepared to share you. I am prepared, Jan."

"Then prepare me," she moaned as she felt his tongue circle her dark rim from behind. "Prepare me for him."

33

Sheikh Darius kissed her between her buttocks once more and then pulled back, still holding her rear cheeks apart. She tasted like a flower, he thought. Clean and pure, untouched and virgin. The sight of her tight rear bud coated in his saliva made his cock flex so hard Darius wasn't sure he could hold back his orgasm much longer. The animal inside wanted to push himself into that forbidden space, feel her opening up for him, hear her scream as he forced his way into her asshole and came with all his power, flooding her canal and staking his claim to her in every way possible.

I was first, and I will always be first to her, he thought as he gritted his teeth when he saw Ephraim lean over and massage the top of her crack, just above where Darius was holding her open. Jan knows it, and this is her attempt to create a balance between us. She understands that Ephraim's ego has different needs from mine, that although we are both proud and stubborn, unyielding and dominant, we are also different men at the heart of it.

Darius glanced up at Ephraim, wondering if the

younger Sheikh would break into a mocking smile. But Ephraim was stoic, rigid with arousal, and when he returned the gaze, Darius saw a spark of something that he himself was feeling. He could sense both their cocks getting harder at the same time, that age-old instinct that gets activated when men are sharing one woman, and he knew this would create a bond between them that even a thousand hours of talking would never accomplish.

"Move back, Ephraim," Darius muttered as he watched Ephraim's fingers move closer to Jan's asshole. "Not yet, my brother. I will prepare her for you. For your entry." He glanced into Ephraim's eyes again. "Entry to which both she and I yield first rights."

Ephraim hesitated for a moment, his eyes darting to Darius's ramrod-straight cock, which was lined up just right. All Darius would have to do was push forward and he would be inside her before either of them could stop him. He could claim her if he wanted. He could invade that space, take it from Ephraim, take it for himself.

The two Sheikhs locked eyes for a long moment, and then finally Ephraim nodded and lifted his hands from Jan's buttocks, backing away on his knees and then going down on his haunches and taking a breath.

"As you say, brother," he said, his jaw tight. "If you can control yourself, then I can as well."

Silence fell upon the three players as the sun moved up in the sky. Jan could smell the pure coconut oil mixing with the aroma of her sex and the scent of the two men. She gasped as Darius slid his middle finger into her anus and carefully slicked her up from the inside, preparing her for his rival. Then she held her breath when Darius withdrew his finger and moved back, parting her rear cheeks one last time before making way for Ephraim.

"Go ahead, Ephraim," she heard Darius say behind her, and the sensation of one king offering her up-turned ass to another was almost too filthy to believe. Was this real? It had to be. It was too insane to be make-believe!

Ephraim was silent, but Jan could feel him move closer to her. She could sense his heavy breathing. She could almost feel the weight of his need.

"She is perfect," said Ephraim finally, and Jan wasn't sure if the Sheikh was speaking to Darius or to her. Perhaps to nobody. "Ya Allah, she is perfect!"

"She is ours," came Darius's reply, and now Jan caught sight of Darius stepping back and circling around to her front. He caressed her hair and she breathed feverishly from the anticipation, and with a warm smile he held her head against his body as Ephraim pressed the swollen head of his cock to her rear entrance.

"Oh, God, I don't know if it'll go," gasped Jan, her eyes going wide when she realized how much she'd have to open up to take Ephraim's shocking girth.

"You were made to take me," whispered Ephraim

from behind her. "To take both of us. See, already you are opening up. By God, this feels exquisite. So smooth. So goddamn tight. Ya Allah, I am so hard for you, my queen."

Jan's mouth opened wide as Ephraim pushed his shaft past her rear opening and into her anus. Darius had prepared her well, and the passage was smooth. Jan tensed up for a moment, her ring tightening around Ephraim's cock and making him groan loudly. But he kept pushing, massaging her rump as Darius caressed her hair and held her face close to his chest. Finally she relaxed, and with a final push Ephraim was all the way inside. All the way deep. All the way hers.

Slowly he pumped, each stroke opening her rear canal in a way that made her gurgle and gasp against Darius's hard body. She could feel Darius's cock hard against her breasts as Ephraim fucked her ass with increasingly powerful strokes, and soon all three of them were in an erotic rhythm that seemed to be in time with the waves lapping at the shores of the Golden Oasis. Jan could see Darius's long cock sliding back and forth between her breasts as Ephraim took her from behind, and when Ephraim finally came inside her, his semen pouring into the farthest reaches of her anus, Darius immediately pulled away from her and circled around.

"Oh, God," Jan groaned when she felt Ephraim pump the last of his load into her with a guttural cry that shook the earth beneath them. And then suddenly he was out of her and Darius was inside, pumping away immediately. "Oh, God, what's happening?"

The switch happened so quick Jan didn't completely realize it until Darius was coming, and then suddenly it all became clear, that both Sheikhs had just finished inside her, one after the other.

34

One thing follows another, thought Ephraim's driver as he took one last look at the contents of the car's trunk. The car was not from the Sheikh's fleet. It was unmarked and unremarkable. Generic and almost invisible.

The sun was close to setting, and the driver laid out his prayer mat and faced Mecca, bowing his head and calling out the prayers that he knew would be his last. Would he end up in heaven or in hell after this act? Was it an act of treason or patriotism? Was he a terrorist or a hero? Only Allah would decide. And the time for decision had come.

The driver finished his prayer and rolled his mat up for the last time, placing it in the empty passenger's seat of the car. Then he started the engine and slowly drove past the capital city of Habeetha, toward the north shores of the Golden Oasis, to the military cantonment, where a hundred-thousand restless young men were polishing their weapons and gazing across the shimmering waters towards Noramaar.

"This is the only way," the driver whispered as he

raced the engine and clicked the timer which activated the bomb in the trunk of the car. "If Sheikh Ephraim will not start this war, then I will. Allah-hu-Akbar. May God forgive me."

35

"**B**y Allah, give them the order to pull back or else I will slit your throat right here, Ephraim!"

"Not until I know what is happening, Darius!" roared Ephraim. "My military barracks has been attacked. A bomb has gone off. It is an act of war. How do I know you didn't plan this to force my hand?"

"Because I am not insane!" shouted Darius, still on the phone with his Council of Ministers, trying on the one hand to calm his generals down while on the other to calm himself down.

Both Sheikhs had gotten phone calls at almost the same time, with Ephraim getting a report that his undisciplined army was already mobilizing to cross the Golden Oasis and attack Noramaar in retaliation for what in their mind was an unprovoked act of war. Darius's Council had called with the news that they were sending out armed boats to intercept Ephraim's fleet before they landed on Noramaar's shores. Suddenly it was war, and no one seemed to know what the hell was going on!

"I knew I could never trust your ambition," growled

Darius, pulling on his shirt and shaking his head in fury. As he grabbed his belt from the ground near the smoldering campfire, his gaze rested on the black box he'd brought with him, and without thinking he snatched it up and flipped it open. He pulled out one of the pistols and cocked the hammer, pointing it squarely at Ephraim and gritting his teeth. "I should end this right now."

Ephraim straightened to full height, tossing his phone to the ground and glancing at the second pistol, which was still in the case. "Are we going to make it a fair duel, or do you want to simply pull the trigger like a coward?" He snorted. "At least that will prove that you did in fact order the cowardly attack on my troops during the evening prayer."

Darius closed his eyes tight, feeling his finger tighten on the trigger. But he couldn't do it, and with a roar he hurled the gun into the bushes and reached for the two daggers. He tossed one into the dirt by Ephraim's feet and raised the other. "Pick it up," he snarled, beginning to circle like an animal. "Pick it up, Ephraim."

Ephraim's jaw set tight as he held eye contact with the circling Sheikh. Then in a lightning move he dived for the dagger in the dirt, grabbing it and rolling toward Darius, slicing at his knees.

Darius leaped out of the way just in time to avoid getting slashed, and then the fight was on. Jan came stumbling out from the guest house just in time to see the two Sheikhs smash into each other, daggers raised, green eyes wild with anger.

"What the hell is happening?!" she screamed, rushing over to them and then quickly stepping back when she saw the glint of steel as the two Sheikhs wrestled for supremacy. Darius had already drawn blood with a slash to Ephraim's upper arm, but Ephraim had parried with a slicing uppercut that had Darius staggering backward and touching his side. "Stop it! Both of you! Have you lost touch with reality?! Stop!!"

But either they couldn't hear or they didn't give a damn, because they were locked again in combat, both of them gripping the other's knife-hand, sweat dripping from their brows and torsos as they grunted and groaned in the sun. At the point of near-despair, Jan looked around for help, for anything. Then she saw the remaining gun, still sitting there in the black case, and she grabbed it.

"I'll shoot both of you if you don't stop this madness right goddamn now!" she shrieked pointing the gun at Darius and then Ephraim. When they didn't notice, she pointed the gun past them and pulled the trigger twice, shattering the silence with the crash of gunfire.

This got their attention, and the two Sheikhs broke away from each other and stared at her in shock. Then they looked at one another, finally down at themselves. They were both soaked in sweat, streaks of blood from their wounds all over their heaving bodies. It was by no means clear whose blood was whose, and so Jan kept the gun pointed at them until they both dropped their weapons.

"OK, talk," she said firmly, nodding at Darius. "You first. What in God's name just happened? I leave you two alone for an hour, and you decide to stab each other to death?"

Darius stayed quiet for a long moment, and then he burst out laughing. A moment later Ephraim joined in, and it was the laughter of madness. Jan waited while the two Sheikhs let the adrenaline subside, and then she listened as they told her what had just happened back in Habeetha. She listened, and then she stared at the two Sheikhs, both of whom were looking at her as if she needed to resolve this, as if this was her first test. Her first test as queen.

"You know," she muttered, shaking her head and finally lowering the gun. "I was hoping we'd have a few months to work out the details, get a better sense of how this was going to work, make careful plans for the wedding. But it looks like we're going to have to accelerate things."

Both Sheikhs were frowning, and Jan sighed and shook her head, folding her arms beneath her breasts and shaking her head again. "So right now both your armies are racing across the Golden Oasis in boats, right?"

"Yes," said Darius.

"Correct," said Ephraim.

"And aren't we on an island in the middle of that same oasis right now?" said Jan.

"If you are suggesting we intercept them ourselves, that is ridiculous," said Darius. "Ephraim's army is un-disciplined and whipped into a frenzy by this bomb-ing. Who is to say they will not simply cut us down in their rage?" He turned to Ephraim. "Even if I am to believe you that the bomb was not trickery on your part, do you believe that you can stop your madmen from seeking vengeance, now that they have blood in their hearts?"

Ephraim took a breath, his jaw tight as he rubbed his stubble. He stayed silent, then quickly shook his head. "It is best if I go alone," he said quietly. "Per-haps I can fly the flag of Habeetha and stop them long enough to reason with them. Perhaps I can—"

"And perhaps you will instead simply join your men and lead them in battle," snorted Darius, shak-ing his head as doubt and mistrust clouded his eyes. "No. We both go. At least if there is to be fighting, it will happen on the water, where our civilians will be safe. He glanced toward where their two yachts were bobbing gently some distance away from the shore. Then Darius pointed at Jan. "You stay here. There are enough supplies, and we will come back for you."

Jan's eyes went wide. "You're joking. No way in hell am I staying on some snake-infested island while you boys are destroying my kingdom before it's even my kingdom!"

Darius and Ephraim both turned to look at her.

"Your kingdom?" said Ephraim, frowning deep.

"Your kingdom . . ." said Darius, his voice lengthening to a drawl as he stared into Jan's eyes.

"You never let me finish what I was saying," said Jan.

"And what were you going to say?" said Darius. "Finish. Please."

"Finish. That's exactly the right word. It's time to finish this. Tie it up. Tie the knot." Jan blinked hard and smiled. "This entire scheme was thought up to prevent a war, wasn't it? And now, when a war has all but begun, you abandon the plan without a second thought. Marriage is about commitment, boys. It's about follow-through. It's about communication, determination, and the will to stay the course."

"There will be plenty of time to worry about that," Ephraim grunted, starting off towards the shoreline and the dingy. "Right now we have a crisis to deal with."

"And so we'll deal with it. All three of us. We give both your kingdoms something new, something dramatic, something that will blow them out of the water," Jan said, leaning forward in her excitement. "We give them their new queen."

36

And as the two fleets closed in on each other in the wide open Golden Oasis, one large yacht flying the flags of both Habeetha and Noramaar swooped in between them, the boat's loudspeaker blaring in Arabic, the voices of both Sheikhs coming through loud and clear across the shining waters.

Both Darius and Ephraim spoke quickly as their war-vessels pulled up and circled the single boat, armed men staring in confusion at the two Sheikhs standing side by side, an American woman between them. By then Darius had spoken to his attendant, the woman who'd washed Jan's feet. The attendant confessed that she'd spoken to Ephraim's driver, and when Ephraim could not reach his driver, they all figured out what must have happened. But this was not the time to reason with hordes of angry young men. The only way to placate them was with a visual spectacle.

So Darius and Ephraim stalled things long enough for a chopper to arrive overhead, and everyone—Jan included—watched in awe as two clerics and several attendants were lowered down onto the deck of the boat. And then both armies watched in muted shock as the attendants draped Jan in wedding silks and the clerics began reciting the prayers of the nikaah ceremony, right there on the ancient waters of the Golden Oasis.

It took some time for the men to realize what was happening, and murmurs rose up on both sides of the fleets. But the clerics represented both Habeetha and Noramaar, and there could be no doubt that the two men on the boat were indeed their supreme Sheikhs. The armies were frozen in place, the confusion taking the fight out of them. How could they go to war when their rulers were standing together and partaking in what had to be the strangest wedding ceremony in the Islamic world!

"From this moment on," said Sheikh Darius when the ceremony was done. He took Jan's hand in his and waited until Ephraim took her other hand.

"Yes, from this moment on," said Ephraim, smiling wide and raising his free hand to the sky. "We are all one. One nation. One kingdom. One people."

"And one family," whispered Jan as she stared in disbelief at the scene around her, men cheering on boats, battleflags flying, the wind wailing, herself in the grip of two kings, two Sheikhs, two husbands. "One family."

∞

EPILOGUE
<u>ONE MONTH LATER</u>

The news spread across the globe like a forest-fire in summer, and the reaction was overwhelming, far beyond their wildest expectations. Even the naysayers from Habeetha and Noramaar could not deny that the unprecedented three-way wedding had elevated the Sheikhs and their kingdoms to a level beyond that of mortal celebrities. Tourism skyrocketed, hundreds of couples wanted to get married on the shores of the Golden Oasis, debates about why it was about time shared marriages like this were accepted and celebrated raged on every medium from daytime talk shows to the editorial pages of theTimes and Post.

Jan had been right in that she was a queen in name only. Naturally she wasn't prepared in the least to actually run a kingdom in an unfamiliar land. The citizens knew this, but that didn't stop them from getting caught up in the global frenzy and embracing her as their own. As for the Sheikhs, well, there was one minor detail to work out. One minor . . . bump, so to speak:

"I'm pregnant," Jan told them that evening when the attendants had cleared the dinner table and left the two Sheikhs and the Sheikha alone. "The Royal doctors informed me this evening."

Both Ephraim and Darius glanced at one another and then back at Jan. She could see the tracings of both joy and apprehension on their handsome faces, and she thought back to the strange argument they'd had over who would be "first" husband.

Then Jan thought back to her own decision when she'd heard of their agreement that the first to father an heir with her would be first husband. Yes, her decision, which was based on something she'd read about the ancient hunter-gatherer tribes and how they'd managed to live peacefully in societies where every woman openly lay with multiple men of the tribe.

"Did you know that certain tribes believed that every child actually had more than one biological father?" Jan said slowly, taking a breath and looking at her two husbands. "No, seriously. After all, there was no way to biologically determine paternity, like we can these days. And it was that lack of knowledge that actually strengthened the bonds between generations of those tribes . . . because no one could be sure whose child was whose."

Ephraim frowned and shifted in his chair. "What are you saying, Jan?"

"No," said Darius, standing up and beginning to pace. "You cannot be serious."

"I am serious," said Jan. "It's the only way. This is the only way we survive as a family."

"It is not done," said Darius. "A child must know who its father is."

Jan touched her belly and glanced up at Darius and then at Ephraim, who seemed to be getting it now—judging by the color of his face. "Our child will always know who its father is. You. And you. Both of you. There can be no other answer. There will be no other answer."

Ephraim laughed, his eyes darkening as he rubbed his chin and stood up. Now both Sheikhs were pacing around the long table, and Jan watched them. She knew this wouldn't be easy, but it was the only way. She had to hold her ground. It was the only way she could balance the egos of these two powerful men. There would be more children, she knew, and she was determined that each child would look to both these men as his or her father. The real father.

She watched as the two of them sulked and grumbled, shouted and stamped. Ephraim swore he'd extract blood himself and get them tested. Darius agreed and said he'd hold her down while Ephraim did it. But Jan stayed strong. This was her body and her decision. They would come around. They had to come around.

"Both of you," she said again. "Both of you will be the real fathers to each child I bear. Both of you. We're one family, and that's how it will be. One family. One blood. One tribe. Always and forever."

And when she saw the mixture of both rage and recognition on their faces, Jan knew that this marriage would always be an experiment. It would always be a game. It would always be unpredictable.

Just like it would always be the three of them. Always and forever.

Always and forever.

∞

FROM ANNABELLE WINTERS

Thanks for reading.

Join my private list at **annabellewinters.com/join** to get steamy epilogues, exclusive scenes with side characters, and a chance to join my advance review team.

And do write to me at **mail@annabellewinters.com** anytime. I really like hearing from you.

Love,
Anna.

Printed in Poland
by Amazon Fulfillment
Poland Sp. z o.o., Wrocław

58957158R00146